Tread Softly,
My Heart

Tread Softly, My Heart

Stella Ross

First Published 1987

First Published in this edition 1990
Published by Russell, Geddes & Grosset
Windsor Court, New York, N.Y.
U.S.A.

ISBN 1 85534 109 3

Printed and bound in Canada

1

"Left, did you say?" Laurel asked in surprise. "But that's impossible. My sister would have been in touch to let me know."

"Nevertheless," Frau Lindt's voice came back high-handedly, "your sister left three weeks ago. And I'm afraid I can give you no forwarding address."

"Oh – er – " Laurel was so taken aback that she couldn't think what to say next.

Frau Lindt solved the problem for her.

"I am sorry, I have got other things to do. I must go now. Goodbye, Miss Brownridge."

"No – wait – " Laurel pleaded. "Do you happen to have the telephone number of the clinic where she works?"

"I am sorry – no. And I really must go. Please excuse me."

The phone was put down at the other end, leaving Laurel to stare at it, still too surprised to take the news in.

Why on earth had her twin sister changed her lodgings in Cologne without even giving her a call to let her know? There *was* a time when they'd confided everything to each other.

She consulted the calendar. When was the

last time they'd been in touch? Good Lord – it must have been all of a month ago. She remembered – it was the evening Gavin had come around to collect the last of his things. Jenny had called wanting to chat but Laurel had said she'd call her back. Her heart had been too full of misery to want to discuss anything at that heart-breaking time.

Now that she could say Gavin's name in her mind without wanting to sink into a well of despair, she could feel appalled at the length of time that had passed before she'd had the good manners to return her sister's call. No wonder Jenny had thought she hadn't cared, and had left her lodgings without letting her know.

But where was she? And had she also left the clinic? She'd have to find out. But that was impossible – she didn't even have the proper address. She'd only been there once, when she'd gone to visit Jenny soon after her twin had taken up the position of nurse manager in Germany.

The rest of Laurel's evening was used up ineffectually with worrying about her sister's whereabouts. She racked her brain incessantly but could think of no one she could call to find out.

When midnight came and went she realized there was little she could do that night. If she managed to get a good night's rest an idea might come to her in the morning. Tomorrow was Saturday and she would have the whole of the weekend to herself. Derrick Hanley, her partner at the fashion shop, had offered to take over some of her responsibilities, since it had become noticeable to him, as well as to the staff they employed, that she'd been working herself to death since the break-up of her engagement to Gavin.

But the good night's sleep she'd hoped for didn't materialize. Instead, it was filled with nightmares. All the childhood misfortunes that had ever struck her sister in the past returned to haunt Laurel. Even to the inclusion of a mysterious, sinister stranger in a trilby hat whom she had never set eyes on before.

When she awoke, hag-ridden with fears for Jenny's safety, it was with the clear knowledge of what she had to do. She must call in and speak to Derrick, to see if he could manage their joint business for longer than just the weekend – at least until she could fly to Cologne, locate her sister and return to England, safe in the knowledge that Jenny was all right.

The moment she walked through the smart doorway of the London fashion shop that had taken her and Derrick two years of hard effort to build into a lucrative and successful business, she incurred his wrath.

"Laurel – what the hell are you doing in this morning? I thought we agreed you were to take things easy for a while? Look at you – you've lost at least fourteen pounds over the past month. You're even thinner than some of the models we employ – "

"I told you I'm all right. You really mustn't worry yourself about me. I'm fine. Completely over Gavin. Finished, finished – finished – "

"Then what are you doing here, when I expressly told you to take the weekend off while I kept an eye on things?"

She kissed his cheek affectionately. They had been friends for seven years – since she was twenty-one. No hanky-panky between them. They just weren't attracted sexually. She knew, if she could ever have had a brother, she might have chosen Derrick. Firm, good-tempered, stable. A perfect foil to her own, somewhat impetuous character, since she'd been blessed with the sort of fiery temperament that often went with people who had her color auburn hair.

"Listen," she told him. "I called Jenny last night and got a nasty shock. She's changed her lodgings. I haven't a clue where she is. And I'm worried, Derrick. Terribly worried. She could be anywhere. I don't even know whether she's still at the clinic. And I can't call her there – I'm not sure of the address." She paused, her hazel eyes wide with alarm. "I'm going quietly frantic. It's been a month since we've had any contact. We've never left it so long before. What I wanted to know is – would you be a dear and extend the weekend you've persuaded me to take off to something longer?"

"How long? We've got a show coming up shortly, remember?"

"I've honestly no idea. However long it takes to find out she's all right and that I'm going out of my mind needlessly."

His face broke into a smile. "Take as long as you like. It's been ages since you've had anything like a real break. I can cope quite well, as you know. You're not nearly as indispensable as you like to suppose."

"Don't thing you can get rid of me *that* easily. It may only take the weekend. I pray it *will* only take the weekend."

"Then if it does, stay over there a couple of weeks, anyway. Have a vacation. God knows, you deserve it."

"I'll give the matter some thought. In the meanwhile I have to book a flight. I wonder, would you do that for me while I slip back to the apartment and pack? I wanted to check it was OK with you before I went that far."

"Surely! Go home and get some things together. I'll come around and pick you up to take you to the airport as soon as I've made the arrangements."

"You're a dear. What would I do without you?"

"You'll never need to try. I've got a very worthwhile niche in life with Laureder Fashions."

Three hours later, resting her head against the back of the seat in the small Lufthansa aircraft, Laurel allowed herself to unwind. She no longer felt worried or apprehensive – just exhausted. The last hours had been hectic with what seemed like a thousand and one things to see to before she could leave her apartment. Derrick had finally got her to the airport with only a few minutes to spare before she was ushered through Passport Control and on to the plane.

Glancing around, she saw one or two of the seats were still empty. They were arranged in threes and she'd been allotted one in the center of a row.

She was fully aware that the nervous-looking middle-aged man who occupied the seat next the window was anxious to start up a conversation. She would have much preferred to remain quiet, but had to feign interest while he chatted on, going into details about the reason he was traveling to Cologne, and expecting to be let into her reason, too.

She was spared from telling him by the arrival of a young man shortly before take-off. He entered the aircraft in a hurry, looked around, and chose to sit in the empty seat on the other side of her.

He was well over six feet tall, and had immense difficulty fitting his long legs under the seat in front. After he'd apologized several times for kicking her, she glanced down at her tights, hoping he hadn't laddered them. Finally, after getting into a hopeless muddle with both their seat belts, confusing hers with his, he settled down.

She faced the front, hoping the hour-long journey wasn't going to be peppered with further ignominious tussels with him. At another period of her life – if she hadn't still been suffering from the after-effects of a broken engagement – she might have found him immensely attractive. He was dark-haired with clear blue eyes and an engaging grin. But his looks reminded her too much of Gavin.

When he began to make tentative overtures toward friendly conversation in a voice that held a slightly transatlantic accent, she ignored them, giving him a tight look of disapproval before pointedly glancing away.

Their plane taxied along the runway before gathering speed and ascending sharply into the clouds. A few moments later it emerged into bright summer sunshine and they were flying over mountains of temptingly soft-looking woolly cumulus clouds. Between gaps she made out the Thames and its tributaries far below. A short while later they were crossing the English Channel.

When the blond stewardess came around to see if everyone was all right, the young man ordered himself a drink. He asked Laurel if she'd like one, too. But she shook her head and distantly mouthed a refusal.

Closing her eyes, she hoped she might dissuade both the men on either side of her from becoming nuisances. She could tell the middle-aged man was itching to continue with his life story, after being silent for only as long as it had taken the plane to level out. And now he had regained his confidence and was asking her where he'd left of.

Soon after the German stewardess had served the young man with his scotch on the rocks in a plastic glass, they hit an unexpected air pocket. The plane dipped and swayed alarmingly, and Laurel opened her eyes in horror as she felt the contents of the glass land icily in the lap of the expensive model dress she'd chosen to wear.

"God – I'm terribly sorry," he apologized. "Don't move – I'll fetch a wad of paper napkins."

She surveyed the damage.

"I shouldn't bother," she said frostily. "My dress is ruined."

"Then, at least let me help you up."

She pushed his hands away exasperatedly, getting to her feet on her own and not daring to look down at the damage a second time. Her mind recoiled. It had been a Kurtfeld model! Appallingly expensive. One she'd tried to resist the temptation of buying and failed, much to the detriment of her bank balance – even at wholesale price. And now, because of the young man's clumsiness, it was completely ruined.

She heard him click his tongue in a sympathetic fashion.

"Gosh – what a shame. The material seems to be puckering up. Should it do that? Have you got anything else you can wear?"

She glared at him. "No – the material shouldn't be puckering up. And, as to your second question, how can I have anything else to wear when my baggage is in the hold like everyone else's?"

She was feeling almost ready to burst into tears, when she suddenly remembered the cotton shirt and shabby jeans she'd stuffed into her hold-all at the last minute. For some curious, but face-saving, reason, as it now appeared, she had stuffed them in, thinking they might come in useful if she had to rough it anywhere in Germany.

The hold-all was above her in the rack. The young man retrieved it for her and she snatched it away from him ungraciously.

"I'm terribly sorry – " he repeated as she hurried in the direction of the toilet.

When she returned some time later, feeling untidy and out of place among the rest of the passengers who were mainly business people, she chose another vacant seat further along, and ignored the man who'd been the cause of her discomfort.

He seemed to get the message and made no further attempt to apologize. The last part of the journey proceeded without further incident.

2

As she had nothing to declare, Laurel was hustled through German Customs competently and quickly. At just gone one, with her large case and hold-all, she was waiting outside for a taxi. As the first one came into view she hailed it.

At the same moment, the young man who'd caused her so much annoyance on the plane, burst through the airport doorway and strode long-leggedly toward it, reaching it a moment before her.

She felt furious, and in no mood to let him claim it as his.

"If you don't mind," she said scathingly, "that taxi is mine. I've just taken the trouble to hail it."

He looked down at her in an amused fashion which annoyed her all the more.

"Oh, really," he drawled. "Well, I happen to have hailed it, too."

"You're a fibber," she accused. "You were nowhere in sight. You came striding through the doors at the last possible moment. I'd already seen it in the distance and put up my hand."

He grew magnanimous. "I tell you what – to save further argument I'll let you share *my* taxi."

"*Mine*!" she seethed.

"OK – have it your way. I'll share *your* taxi."

"Oh, no, you won't. Are you going to move out of the way and let me get my things in, or are we going to stay here all day bickering?"

As they were arguing another taxi came into view. He saw it before she did.

"Very well – you win. I never could bear hassling with domineering females."

"I'm *not* domineering," she began angrily but he didn't seem to be listening.

Relinquishing his hold on the door, he put up a hand and hailed the other taxi, making for it smartly before anyone else had the chance. Just as it stopped by his side he threw over his shoulder –

"I've only ever seen you when you're sore, but I'd like to tell you how attractive I think you are – even in those old jeans. Do you know, temper has a habit of making your hazel eyes sparkle like gems."

The unexpected compliment made her turn and stare at him in surprise. But a moment later she tossed her head and pushed him out of her thoughts before she gave the driver her instructions.

"The Raspeig Hotel in Jacobsdummer Strasse, please."

Within a quarter of an hour she was there

and paying the man off. Moments later she heaved her case and hold-all through the door of the small hotel.

Frau Lindt received a shock at first, then realized she was the other Miss Brownridge.

"I'm afraid you've had a wasted journey," she said in her guttural accent. "I thought I made it clear last evening that I had no idea where your sister might be – "

"That's so – but I came all the same. I need to find out where she's moved to. I intend to make inquiries at the clinic where she works. In the meantime I thought, if you had a room, I could stay here, at least for one night."

The woman became slightly more affable. "You are welcome. I happen to have one spare room. It was your sister's. You may stay there the night."

"That's kind of you."

"Come, I will show you. You may leave that heavy case here in the hall until my man comes back on duty."

"Don't worry – I can manage it," said Laurel, struggling as she followed the fat *Frau* up to Jenny's small room on the first floor where she had visited her that last time.

After Frau Lindt had unlocked it, she remembered something.

"Ah, I have a haversack of your sister's that she has left behind. I put it into this cupboard in the hall. I will give it to you to return to her."

"A haversack!"

The woman shrugged. "Your sister bought it last winter when she went to Switzerland for the winter sports. One moment – "

She opened the cupboard and handed Laurel the small, blue haversack.

"There are some old clothes that I found in her closet and put inside," she said fastidiously. "I could not leave them about where they might contaminate other people's things."

"Thank you, Frau Lindt," Laurel said tautly.

If this dreadful woman had behaved so rudely when Jenny was living there, no wonder she'd been unable to stand it and had left. But she should have had the sense to let her know.

Sinking down on the bed and kicking off her uncomfortable high-heeled shoes, she wondered where she should start in her search. It was lunch-time, but she wasn't at all hungry.

Undoing the straps of the haversack, she turned its contents on to the bed. There was a sweater that had seen better days. And a funny old bobble-hat Jenny must have worn when she went skiing.

Several other odd bits of clothing were among the jumble. They were all old, as Frau Lindt had said. But they were clean.

She picked up a green blouse, that had once been hers before she'd given it to Jenny. Something bulged in the top pocket. Inside she found a photograph and a folded-up cutting from a newspaper.

The photo was of Jenny with a good-looking man. They were laughing with each other in the snow. It had evidently been taken on her skiing holiday.

Jenny had always had many more boyfriends than Laurel. Laurel had always been the serious one. Long ago, when they were in their teens, their mother had had a habit of introducing them to her friends, not as twins, but as her pretty daughter and her brilliant one. It had peeved Laurel slightly until her mother had explained that she had always wanted them to have separate identities, and that was the reason she had always refrained from dressing them alike.

As Laurel flipped the snap over, she saw, written in Jenny's handwriting – *Me with Erich, before we really knew each other. And now, so much in love, it hurts.*

The inscription came as a surprise. She had never known Jenny to write anything so emotional about anyone before. Maybe this man was someone special. Laurel unfolded the cutting taken from a German newspaper. On one side there were small advertisements – mostly hospital vacancies. On the other side was just a picture of a large mansion. Underneath was written its name – Hohengrünfeld – and the name of the nearby town – Stuttgart.

Laurel went downstairs, taking the photo

and cutting with her. Frau Lindt was in the hall chatting to some German teenagers in hiking gear who had evidently just arrived back for lunch. As soon as they'd disappeared hungrily into the dining-room, she showed her the photograph.

"I'm sorry to bother you, but can you tell me who this is and whether you know his address? He might know where my sister's moved to."

Frau Lindt gave it a quick cursory glance before shrugging her shoulders.

"Your sister had many men-friends. I can't say I recall seeing this person. Always she entertained them away from the hotel. I do not permit any of my guests to take persons of the opposite sex up to their rooms."

She picked up the magazine she'd been reading on top of the reception counter and turned away. Laurel felt frustrated. The woman was being so deliberately unhelpful for some season that she wished she hadn't booked to stay for that night. But she knew Cologne so little, and the hotel was near to the railway station if she had to go deeper into Germany.

Swiftly she made up her mind to change and try to find the clinic where Jenny worked. If she was there all the time, it would save any more anxiety. She had no reason to suppose she'd given up her work as well as her room. What reason would she have to do that?

As she started up the stairs again, Frau Lindt called after her.

"I wonder, Miss Brownridge, if you have considered the possibility that your sister may have been in some kind of trouble – pregnant perhaps? She appeared to put on a little weight in the past month, and – as I have already said – she had many boyfriends."

The remark was so uncalled for that Laurel's color rose with indignation.

"There's not the remotest chance of that, I can assure you, Frau Lindt. If you remember, my sister's job is a nurse manager. For that she had to qualify as a nursing sister. She's well acquainted with the facts of life. I've no doubt, if the situation had ever arisen, she would have known quite well how to protect herself.

As Laurel continued up the stairs, the nagging thought crept in that the woman might be right. It would account for the fact that Jenny had left without telling her where she was going. She might have felt too ashamed and upset. It would also account for the fact that she'd been eager to chat, that time a month ago.

No. It wasn't possible. Not Jenny. She shook the thought away. Of the two of them Jenny had always been the least emotional. She would never be likely to get into such a situation.

Then the wording on the back of the photo flew back – *so much in love it hurts*.

She compressed her full lips so that her firm, white chin jutted determinedly. If that was the case, it was even more essential that she found out where Jenny was to lend all her support.

Changing into a turquoise-colored suit that made her auburn hair gleam like satin, she left the hotel and walked toward the corner of the road.

It was no use hailing a taxi, she decided. As much as she racked her brains she couldn't think of the clinic's name or in which direction it lay. All she could remember was that Jenny had taken her there once by bus. It was possible that, from the top deck of the vehicle, if it had one, she might recognize her whereabouts.

If she didn't, she had nothing to lose. It would then be a matter of looking up the names of every clinic in the local telephone directory and seeing whether any of them struck a chord in her memory.

The *Hältstelle,* she remembered, was close to the cathedral. A bus came along shortly after she reached it. It was a single decker and full except for two places. She hesitated. And then her mouth opened in surprise as she recognized a voice that spoke from directly behind.

"Well – if it isn't little 'Ruby Redhead.' "

She turned. "Oh, no – not you," she said fiercely, staring up into the amused face of the young man she'd met on the plane.

"Hurry along, there," said the driver in German.

"Now – do as the nice man says," he

grinned, giving her a small prod that propelled her into the vehicle in front of him.

After they'd purchased tickets he sat down in the vacant seat next to her.

Leaning over, he said, in an intimate tone – "Now, tell me – do you believe in fate?"

"If you don't mind," she said sharply, "I'd prefer to pretend you don't exist. I don't want anything else spilt over me."

He laughed. "Tell me what I've done to deserve your scorn – apart from spilling my perfectly good drink down your perfectly ordinary dress?"

She gave him a look that spoke volumes. "It wasn't an *ordinary* dress. It happened to be a *model* one. And it cost me a great deal of money."

He felt in his pocket and brought out a handful of notes.

"So – allow me to reimburse you for my clumsiness. How much would you like?"

"Please put that away," she said embarrassed, as he tried to press some into her hand. "You're absolutely incorrigible."

"Don't say I'm beginning to wear you down?" He grinned, putting the money back in his pocket. "But now tell me, what's a smart girl like you doing traveling by bus? I thought taxis were more in your line?"

"Don't bother me. I'm trying to keep my mind on where we're going. If you must know, I'm looking for somewhere."

"Like what?"

"A clinic."

"Any idea of its name?"

"If I had, I'd have taken a taxi, wouldn't I?"

"Why don't you ask the bus driver? There can't be many clinics on his route. Are you sure you're on the right bus?"

She became unsure. "Ye-es – I think so. And the reason I can't ask the driver is that I don't speak German. Or, at least, I do – but extremely badly."

As they drew up at a set of traffic lights he said – "Pray let me do something to assist you, ma'am."

In perfect German he spoke to the man in front. The driver replied and he turned back to Laurel.

"That's one problem solved. You get off at the next stop and take the first road on the left. He says the place'll jump out and bite you. You can't miss it."

As soon as they arrived at the next stop she got up, squeezing her way past him.

"Thanks for your help," she said coolly.

He stood up and doffed an imaginary cap. "Not at all, ma'am. Only too happy to oblige. Mayhap we'll meet again if you're staying in Cologne."

"I don't think there's the remotest chance of that," she told him. "Misfortunes rarely happen to me more than three times in a row."

"Oh – one to you!" He laughed. Then, as

she jumped off the bus, he called after her – "You know, you have the most fascinating little dimple nestling close to your chin, Miss Redhead."

She tossed her head, ignoring his wave as the bus drove past.

3

Following the driver's instructions, Laurel took the next road to her left. To her relief, there was the large, white, bay-fronted building, encased in its neat hedging of privet, that she remembered.

She made her way through the gates and toward the reception office.

It was impossible to recall the position of her sister's office. The last time she'd been there with Jenny they'd gone up several staircases and a myriad of corridors until they reached it. Laurel was forced to ask the friendly receptionist if she could direct her there.

The woman smiled, speaking helpfully in English. "You say your sister's name is Brownridge – what is her position here? You see, I am new to the clinic. I have only been here a week and have yet to learn everyone's face by sight."

"Jenny is a nurse manager," Laurel told her. "She has an office here but I can't remember where."

The receptionist consulted a large plan of the building and then flipped through a list of staff names. Finally she gave a shake of her head.

"I am sorry, but the name of the nurse manager appears to be Linda Schmidt – not Jennifer Brownridge."

Laurel gave her a smile that was slightly indulgent. "That's impossible. I think you may have read things wrong. May I have a look? I know my sister works here. I'm perfectly sure I've got the right place."

"Perhaps I am wrong, as you say. But I will call someone else who may know. One moment, please."

Laurel waited in anticipation as she put through a call. A short time later the receptionist replaced the phone giving Laurel a smile.

"There – the mystery is cleared. I have just been told that your sister *did* work here until a few weeks ago, but she has now left."

Laurel's face dropped. "That's bad news. I was banking on finding her here. I don't know where else to look. She's left the place where she was living, as well." A thought struck her. "Is it possible for you to give me the name of her new employer?"

The woman gave a shrug. "I am afraid not. According to the person I inquired from your sister did not leave to take up other employment." She studied Laurel's face thoughtfully. "Perhaps she has returned to England?"

"No – she would have come to my apartment." She frowned anxiously. "I don't understand what's happened to her at all."

The telephone rang and the woman apologized sympathetically before picking it up.

"I am very sorry I can be of so little help. But I am quite sure she will get in touch with you soon. Perhaps, if you have an address in Cologne, you would give it to me. If I have further news I can then let you know. Just let me answer this call first."

She picked up the receiver. The conversation with another official went on for some time. Laurel listened in, trying to brush up her knowledge of the language.

She heard what she thought was – "Well, she didn't leave the building this way. I've been on duty since one – I'd have seen her – "

As the talk went on Laurel lost the thread. But near the end, she heard the woman say – "Very well – I'd better call the number of the doctor attending her, since you say the woman is dangerous – "

When she put the phone down, Laurel asked interestedly – "Problems?"

The woman nodded. "A big one. It seems a woman from the psychiatric unit has absconded. Someone is going to get into a lot of trouble. I'm glad it's not me." She pushed a pen and a piece of paper across the counter. "Now – if you would like to write down your name and address here and in England, I can let you know the moment I hear anything of your sister's whereabouts."

Laurel thanked her.

As she left, she wondered what she could do next. Why on earth was Jenny causing her so much anxiety when just a phone call would have made everything all right?

Then a silly feeling of panic gripped her. What if she'd been kidnapped? It wasn't all that crazy an idea. Idiotic, violent things were happening in the world today.

No – she musn't let herself believe anything so terrible. She must cling to the hope that it was something else that had stopped Jenny from calling.

Frau Lindt's uncomfortable suggestion that Jenny was pregnant returned. Laurel gave a sigh. Well, if it was true it wouldn't be the end of the world.

Damn! – she remembered now. She should have shown someone at the clinic that photograph of Jenny with her boyfriend. They might have recognized him. But, foolishly, she'd left it in her room.

Maybe she was being too complacent. Ought she to inform the German police? But, if she did, they'd probably disregard it. There was no law to say a woman of twenty-eight couldn't leave her lodgings and her job and move wherever she wanted.

She was making too much of things. There was probably a very simple and logical explanation for Jenny's disappearance and she'd no doubt get news from the receptionist at the clinic before long.

Since Derrick had told her to take a holiday she'd comply. She certainly had no stomach to go back to the fashion shop at the moment, before she'd had news that Jenny was safe and well.

When the bus took Laurel back to the city she wandered around until it grew dark, trying to come to a decision about her next move. In the end, feeling slightly peckish for the first time in weeks, she had a light meal in a restaurant before making her way back to Frau Lindt's.

The night was dark, with a moon that kept retiring behind banks of heavy clouds. Fortunately the lights along Jacobsdummer Strasse were bright.

Halfway along, Laurel came to a standstill as she noticed a figure in a long raincoat waiting on the opposite side of the road from the small hotel. For some reason she felt disturbed. There was something about the figure that was oddly familiar, although the major part of the person's face was hidden by a trilby hat.

Remembrance of the dream she'd had in England the night before flew back. This person was surely the same one who'd haunted her nightmare, making her so certain that Jenny was in danger.

She stayed where she was, too apprehensive to move nearer. Then, to her horror, the man left his position and crossed the road. Slowly, and menacingly he moved toward her. Laurel remained rooted to the spot.

The next moment, to her endless gratitude, she heard the teenagers she'd met earlier that evening come through the doors of the hotel, talking and laughing loudly. They were crowded on the sidewalk no more than twenty-five yards away.

Taking her courage in both hands, she moved forward again. What could the stranger possibly do to harm her now, with so many people about?

When they were only a few feet away she caught a look of hatred in his eyes. At the same time, she thought she saw a glint of steel in the hand nearest her.

The man jostled against her as he passed and she gave a gasp as she felt the point of a sharp knife against her ribs.

"Don't think you've seen the last of me," he whispered viciously in German.

"You're mad!" she uttered hoarsely. "What have I ever done to harm you?"

The young Germans had made up their minds where they were going and were all on their way toward them. The man didn't stop but went quickly on his way.

A few moments later she walked shakenly into the hotel, catching sight of her white face in the hall mirror.

What ought she to do – get Frau Lindt to telephone the police? She discarded the thought as soon as it arose. What good would it do? The man was probably streets away by now. If he wasn't crazy he was probably on drugs. Anyway, he'd evidently mistaken her for someone else. And, what she'd thought was a knife was probably something quite different. She was dramatizing everything due to that frightening dream and her worry over her sister.

Far better to go quietly up to her room, crawl into bed, get a night's rest and see how she felt the next morning.

After fearing at first that she may not sleep, due to all the day's excitement, Laurel was fortunate enough to drift off as soon as her head touched the pillow. She slept for a full eight hours, without suffering a single nightmare, and woke feeling refreshed and none the worse for her disturbing encounter of the night before.

The therapeutic effect of a good night's sleep was to make her see things in a more optimistic light. She remembered another lead that she'd forgotten completely about. It was the newspaper cutting that Jenny had left with the photograph.

Picking it up from the bedside table, she studied it again, feeling it must, somehow, be extremely important, since Jenny had taken the trouble to cut it out.

Hohengrüfeld – Stuttgart. A beautiful house

– perhaps connected with the man in the snap with Jenny? But Stuttgart! Her spirits dropped. It was miles away. Was it really possible anyone living there could be of help?

She set her lips determinedly. If there was the remotest chance of it she must leave no stone unturned. It was worth using up a couple of days finding out. There was no sense in staying on in Cologne, wasting her precious holiday by doing nothing decisive.

Making up her mind, she went over to the window to see what sort of day it was. Parting the drapes, she peered out.

The weather was overcast and looked less warm. But that was so much the better for her if she was going to be spending the better part of it cooped up in a train. Then her glance moved downward and she became filled with alarm.

The man who'd accosted her the night before was there again. She closed her eyes tightly and opened them just to see whether he was a figment of her imagination. But he was still there.

Gently she let the drapes fall back into place, praying he hadn't noticed.

How was she possibly going to leave the hotel and make for the station without him seeing? If she ordered a taxi so that she could take her heavy case and her hold-all with her, he would surely realize where she was going and follow her. The station was so close, he'd probably reach it even before she had time to look up a train to her destination.

Her blood ran cold.

Who had he mistaken her for? Perhaps he was a multiple killer or a maniac on the run? But why choose her?

A reckless idea suddenly came into her head as she heard the teenagers in the room next door starting to get up, chattering like monkeys and waking up everyone else.

Yesterday she'd heard them discussing catching a steamer to Koblenz first thing. What if she were to dress up in Jenny's old clothes, stuff what else she could of hers in that haversack, and leave the hotel at the same time as them? The stranger would have a difficult job picking her out.

Her plan made her feel better. She also realized that it would make traveling to Stuttgart and back so much simpler if she didn't have to haul her heavy case with her. Surely Frau Lindt would look after it – especially if she was sufficiently reimbursed!

Toying once more with the idea of phoning the police, she turned it down at once. The man would run a mile if anyone in uniform approached him. And who would believe her story then, that he'd threatened her with a knife? She was a foreigner in another land. It was far better to leave Cologne without calling undue attention to herself.

She slipped on her dressing-gown and went

downstairs to speak to Frau Lindt, gaining her reluctant permission to look after her case until she returned.

Back in her room once more, she dressed in the faded jeans she'd worn the day before, and felt suddenly relieved she'd brought them with her. They'd already got her out of one predicament – when that silly young man on the plane had succeeded in ruining her dress. Maybe they would get her out of an even greater one.

Remembering the young man's impulsive behavior in showering her with compliments, she allowed herself a smile. Another time – another place – if she was entirely honest with herself, she might have enjoyed meeting him again. Why on earth wasn't he around when she'd needed him last evening?

She put the foolish thought aside.

When she donned the blouse she'd given her sister ages ago, it made her look years younger. She studied her reflection thinking how long ago it was since she'd dreamed of going out dressed in such clothes. As joint owner of Laureder she had an image to keep up. She smiled. What on earth would her customers say if they could see her now?

She glanced up at her unusual colored hair. Something would have to be done about that, she thought desperately.

Picking up her last item of disguise – Jenny's idiotic bobble-hat – she dragged it down over her ears, tucking in every vestige of hair.

Looking back at her reflection she made a face. She looked like an escapee from a nut-house. No one who knew her would ever recognize her now.

The teenagers were still having breakfast when she went downstairs. She'd already settled her account with Frau Lindt, and had placed her case in the cupboard that had contained Jenny's haversack. She waited in the sitting-room, unobtrusively.

When the children were ready to leave she was delighted to see that they were dressed surprisingly like herself. Shouting goodbye to their landlady – who was somewhere in the interior – they left in a noisy group. Laurel tagged on behind.

With her heart beating like a drum she kept in step with them as they left the hotel, not daring to even glance at the other side of the road. But, out of the corner of her eye, she could see the man was still there, keeping a watchful eye on everyone who came out. Apparently their departure had caused him little interest as, to her relief, he made no attempt to follow.

Just before they turned the corner, she risked a small peep over her shoulder. He was still standing there in the same position, but, this time, he seemed to be staring up at the room she'd vacated on the first floor.

Feeling slightly jubilant that her plan had worked, she parted company with the teenagers, without them even being aware she'd made use of them. Triumphantly she made for the station.

Purchasing a ticket and studying the timetable of train departures, Laurel saw her train was due to leave Cologne for Stuttgart at nine-forty-five. She found the right platform, took off her haversack, and sat down on a bench.

People were coming and going all around. Most were waiting for the same train. An elderly lady came and sat next to her, nibbling like a mouse at a piece of chocolate she kept hidden in a capacious handbag. A fat girl was laughing and sharing a donut with her equally fat boyfriend.

Laurel regretted the fact that she'd missed her breakfast. But she'd been far too proud to show herself in the dining-room in front of Frau Lindt, once she'd changed into Jenny's old clothes.

After the train had pulled in, the elderly lady scrambled with the best of them for the last seat in one of the coaches. All Laurel managed to get was a place in the corridor. Then she discovered a pull-down seat.

The weather had grown warm and she was dying to pull off her bobble-hat and let her hair free. But she knew it was safer to leave it on, at least until the train moved off and she'd left the sinister stranger well behind.

When they began to get ready to leave she felt an overwhelming feeling of relief. And then flying footsteps made themselves heard along the length of the platform. She held her breath, despairingly, not daring to look out.

Just as the train began to move off, the carriage door nearest her was suddenly thrown open. She cringed. Then a hefty haversack was thrown in. It was closely followed by a long pair of jeans-clad legs and then the whole body.

Laurel froze. She could barely believe her eyes.

The man turned his powerful frame athletically and slammed the door behind him. Without looking at her he said –

"Whew! That was a close one. I nearly missed it."

"What a shame!" she returned sarcastically in English.

He did a double-take before recognizing her. And at once his face broke into a smile.

"Good Lord – not old Ruby Redhead again! I say – you're not following me around, by any chance, are you?"

4

Laurel fought down the curious feeling of delight and pleasure at meeting the same young man again as quickly as it arose.

She kept her tone offhand. "I'd say it was *you* who was doing the following, since *I* happened to be here first."

"Oh, I'm sorry," he said, giving a small bow. "In that case, would you mind very much if I – " he glanced along the corridor and included everyone else – "along with about three hundred or so other passengers, shared your train?"

She turned away refusing to allow him to see that his words amused her. Then she took off Jenny's ridiculous bobble-hat and ran her fingers through her hair.

"That's better," he commented. "You look much more attractive without the comic head piece."

"Do you mind not passing so many personal remarks?" she said coolly.

Feeling behind for a pull-down seat, and finding none, he had to be content with sitting on the floor, drawing his long legs up in front of him, steeple-wise.

"Tell me, what's a guy got to do to get a cordial word out of you?" he asked in a puzzled way. "If I promise not to have a drink in your vicinity – or run for a taxi you've already hailed – or jump on any future vehicle you may catch – do you think it might help you to become a more pleasant traveling companion?"

"I don't intend being your companion for any longer than it takes to reach my destination," she said frostily.

"Oh, and where's that?"

She hesitated for a moment. "Stuttgart."

He gave a look of surprise. "You're joking, surely. You're not really going to Stuttgart, are you?"

"Why shouldn't I?"

His blue eyes twinkled. "Because that happens to be where I'm making for, too." He glanced at his watch. "That gives us – let me see – about five or six hours to get better acquainted." He put out his hand. "I'm Paul Troughton."

It would have been unforgivably rude if she'd refused to shake hands with him. When she did, it was swallowed up almost irretrievably in his firm clasp.

"My name's Laurel Brownridge," she murmured.

He repeated it with a look of pleasure. "Laurel – I like that – it's unusual. Sort of conjures up crowns of evergreen – Roman victors – marathon runners – "

"I'm so relieved you didn't mention Oliver Hardy," she said dryly, reclaiming her hand again after an effort.

He laughed appreciatively. "I like your sense of humor, Laurel. Now – tell me – what are you doing traveling all the way to Stuttgart? And why have you done away with yesterday's suave image?"

She glanced swiftly at his own casual attire.

"I might ask you the same," she challenged.

"Ah – but I asked you first." His grin was engaging. It crinkled up the edges of his deep blue eyes very attractively.

She fought a battle with herself, wondering whether she should confide in him. What was there about him that so much encouraged her trust? Perhaps it was his open, boyish manner, although he was probably two or three years older than her and around thirty.

She frowned. But, in that case, what was he doing dressed shabbily in jeans and carrying camping gear? He hadn't seemed the hitch-hiking type when she'd met him yesterday. His clothes had then been extremely smart.

She came to a decision, asking herself what harm it could possibly do to tell him the truth. For all she knew, he might even be able to help by injecting new ideas.

"If you must know, I'm looking for my sister. I'm hoping to get news of her in Stuttgart."

"How's that? Does she live there?"

Laurel shook her head.

"Why so crestfallen?" he queried sympathetically.

His kindness was all she needed to persuade her to tell him everything that had happened since she'd first tried to call Jenny in Cologne.

When she'd finished he asked to see the newspaper cutting and spent several moments examining it.

"Hohengrünfeld – it certainly looks some place," he said approvingly, handing it back. "But what makes you seriously believe there may be any connection between this *Herrenhaus* and your sister?"

"You're right. There may not be any. It's just a feeling. Knowing Jenny as well as I do, I'm certain she wouldn't have cut it out of the paper without good reason. I'm banking on the fact that the man in the photo I told you about, might live there. If so, Jenny could be there, too."

He smiled. "Then you think she could have run off with her lover?"

"That's always a possibility."

"And what will you do if there's no tie-up at all?"

She sighed. "At the moment I don't even want to think about it. I've nothing else to go on. And I don't think I could face the thought of going back to work and worrying every day about what's happened to her."

He was interested in learning more about her and asked lots of questions about herself and her job. She found it a relief to talk to a stranger about something other than her sister's disappearance.

Eventually, when there was a gap in their conversation, she asked – "And what about you? What kind of work do you do?"

He grew reticent. "I don't. At least, not at the moment. I've just got back from the States. I'm taking time off to acclimatize myself to European ways again."

"Is that what made you catch a plane to Cologne?"

"A part of the reason." He patted the camping gear he carried that looked brand new. "I thought a spot of wandering, before I settled down to something, wouldn't come amiss."

"And why are you making for Stuttgart?"

He raised an eyebrow and laughed. "Hey – what's this? A third degree?"

She colored and looked fixedly out of the window. Why had she been so foolish as to let him see she was interested in him? The moment the train stopped at Stuttgart they would part and go their separate ways. Her heart lost some of its lightness, gained with his company. For some reason she didn't want to pursue the thought.

"What if I said I'd decided to make Stuttgart my jumping-off point?" he said. "As a matter of fact I happen to know someone there." He paused, studying her expression thoughtfully. "In fact – if you press my arm, I might even tag along with you and help you to find your sister – "

She gasped. "I couldn't possibly allow you to use up your holiday helping me."

"Why ever not? I was going to tramp around on my own. We could – sort of – join forces for a while. Kids do it all the time."

She replied more dogmatically. "Neither of us is a child. And, as I say, I can't possibly let you use up your valuable free time on me."

"Very well," he said reluctantly. "Have it your way. At Stuttgart we say goodbye."

The thought depressed her. As though it was mutual, they allowed the subject to drop.

At Heidelberg, for the first time along the journey, more people got off than got on and they were able to find seats in a coach. Paul took her haversack and stowed it with his on the rack.

"I don't suppose you have any food in there, have you?" he asked hopefully. "I don't think we arrive in Stuttgart till about four. And I'm already suffering from my lack of breakfast."

She felt for him, in view of the frame he had to fill.

"I'm sorry – no." She shook her head.

He made up his mind. "Fair enough. Then guard those seats with your life. I'll see if I can buy us some sandwiches. They usually have refreshment trolleys on the platforms, if I remember rightly."

She watched him hurry for the nearest exit.

As he jumped out, she called after him – "Be quick! I've no idea how long the train stops here."

He called back, already out of view.

"I didn't know you cared. Never fear – I'll be back. You can't get rid of me that easily."

It was a relief that he couldn't see her reaction. Her smile was fonder than she might have imagined after so short an acquaintance and she told herself how silly she was being. She was discovering that one of Paul Troughton's greatest attractions was his easy charm. It would be even more foolish, she told herself, if she fell for him on the rebound after her broken engagement.

But, when the train began to move off a few minutes later and he hadn't returned, she jumped to her feet anxiously, to see if she could see him running along the platform.

There was no sign of him, though she scoured the crowds. Her heart dropped.

Then his voice called out from a few yards away.

"I said you couldn't get rid of me that easily, didn't I?"

She could have wept with relief. He had evidently taken the precaution of getting on the train further away and walking along the corridor.

"Here, grab these – " he said, throwing a pack of sandwiches at her. "I've brought one cup of coffee, only. That's all I could carry, so we'll have to share. Don't drink it all."

She followed him into their coach, wondering what she would have done if he'd missed the train. It was unnerving the way she'd begun to rely on him.

At Stuttgart station he gathered their haversacks from the rack, helping Laurel to put hers on. It had grown much warmer. She'd already stripped off Jenny's jumper and was down to jeans and a cotton shirt.

As they stepped on to the platform he stopped and put out his hand. "Well, I guess this is goodbye."

Her face fell. She'd forgotten about her refusal to accept his help. Reluctantly, she shook hands with him, not wanting him to leave, but not daring to ask him to stay. During their time together she'd felt as though she'd come to know him. And now they were strangers again, parting forever in a railroad station.

He studied her expression solemnly before shaking his head.

"Has anyone told you how obstinate you are Laurel?"

She shrugged. "Probably – why?"

"Because it's true. And if you won't ask me – then I'll just have to offer my services again, won't I? But it will be the last time, so watch your reply carefully." He captured her gaze with a serious expression. "Do you want me to help you find your sister or not? Or do you really want to go it alone?"

She turned away, wrestling with her pride.

"Will you help me, please?" she whispered softly.

There was a moment of silence before he replied. "Indeed I will!" The pleasure in his voice rang true. He gave her shoulder a squeeze. "Come on – let's go and give Helga the shock of her life."

"Helga?" she asked, wondering whether she'd heard right.

He nodded. "You remember – the friend I told you about."

"Oh – oh, I see."

For a moment she felt a sharp twinge of jealousy before pushing it firmly away. Somehow she'd assumed the friend he'd mentioned would be male. How idiotic to feel jealous because he'd got a girlfriend there. She reminded herself she'd got no personal claim on him. All he'd done was to offer to help her find Jenny.

But she was thoughtful as they left the station. Then she asked curiously –

"Is Helga your current girlfriend – or just one of your many ex's?"

Her question amused him.

"Neither – she's an old family friend. Believe it or not, Laurel, I don't go crackers over every girl I meet – especially if they happen to be twenty years older."

She felt suddenly light-hearted with relief. Color crept into her cheeks. "I'm very sorry – I didn't know – I shouldn't have asked – "

"Why not – if it interests you?"

"I'm not one bit interested," she parried sharply. "I really couldn't care less how many girlfriends you have."

He teased her. "Ah – that's a shame and I'm terribly disappointed. I'd just begun to fool myself I'd made an impression and now you tell me I'm wrong. Well, I shall just have to drown my sorrows in a cup of Helga's strong tea. If there's one thing she's good at, it's making tea and doling out sympathy – "

Laurel was intrigued to know what sympathy he'd required in the past. But she wasn't going to make the same mistake again of letting him know his past interested her.

The walk took them about a quarter of an hour. Paul told her that Helga lived with her bed-ridden mother on the other side of the beautiful Schlossgarten, with its fountains and theater and attractively laid-out gardens.

"This is it," he said, coming to a halt in front of a small neat villa.

Laurel followed him up the path. Before they reached the end, the door was thrown open by a slim middle-aged woman, who stood there on the threshold, her plain features made almost beautiful by a radiant smile.

"Paul!" she exclaimed – bursting into English with a strong German accent. "What are you doing in Germany? I thought you were still in America. Why didn't you let me know you were coming? I might so easily have been out shopping – "

He wrapped his arms around her in an enormous bear-hug that restrained conversation and almost made her disappear.

"How's my old Helga?" he asked affectionately. "And how's Mutti?"

"Well – oh, very well," she laughed, extricating herself. "And so much better for seeing you." Then she sobered. "And Mutti – well, Mutti's as well as can be expected."

Her eyes suddenly picked out Laurel who'd been partially hidden.

"Oh, but you've brought a companion. How good!"

He introduced them. Then Helga welcomed them indoors.

"Come along in, the pair of you," she said happily, "I'll put the kettle on for a nice cup of English tea."

Paul nudged Laurel and winked conspiratorially as they took off their haversacks in the tiny hall. Then they were ushered up to be introduced to Mutti, a frail, white-haired old lady who lay in bed, partially paralyzed from a stroke.

When they came downstairs again they were both given tea and good-sized portions of home-made cake. As they ate it, Paul told Helga about Laurel's search for her sister.

She shook her head sympathetically.

"This must be extremely upsetting for you. I wonder what the answer can be? Do you think you may learn something from this large *Herrenhaus* – Hohengrünfeld? I know of it – it lies on the edge of the city,."

Laurel brought out the snap that had been taken of her sister during Jenny's winter holiday.

"I'm hoping we'll find that the man in this photo lives there."

Paul, who hadn't seen it before, looked over Helga's shoulder.

"Good Lord – you didn't mention that you and your sister were identical twins." He laughed. "You're like two peas in a pod."

Laurel gave a nod. "So we're often told. And losing her – well it's like losing a piece of myself." She grew nostalgic. "When we were small we even used to get each other's pains. If I fell over it was Jenny who did the crying. And when she broke her arm, mine was in agony for days."

Helga patted her hand. "I do hope you find that this nice-looking man and the person who owns Hohengrünfeld are one and the same person, my dear. How will you go about it? Will you phone there first – or go and see them?"

"I think the personal touch might be best," Paul commented.

"That is very sensible. And you must both

stay here tonight," Helga insisted. "I shall take Laurel upstairs and show her where she can freshen up. She will surely want to change before you go out again."

"That's very kind of you," Laurel said. "But I can quite easily find a small hotel somewhere around here for the night."

"Nonsense – you will take up no more room than Paul," Helga told her.

While she led her upstairs, he helpfully cleared away the tea things, taking them into the minute kitchen.

"Paul tells me you're an old family friend," Laurel said conversationally before they reached the landing.

"Oh, hasn't he told you?" Helga asked in surprise. "I was his family's *au pair* a long time ago. I wanted to learn English so I came to your country. And there I was fortunate enough to obtain employment at their house."

"Oh, I see. Then that accounts for how well he speaks German. I expect you taught it to him."

"Yes, I did," she said proudly. "It was just one of the things I could do in return for all the kindness his family showed me. And do you speak German, too?"

"A little. But I'm too embarrassed to use it, in case my accent is laughed at."

"Oh, you English – you are much too proud. You laugh at foreigners for attempting what you dare not."

As they came out on the landing Laurel wondered where the rest of the bedrooms were. There only appeared to be two – and a bathroom.

"This is where you shall sleep," Helga told her, showing her into the room that was undoubtedly hers. In it there was a comfortable-looking double bed.

"But where will you sleep?" Laurel asked in surprise.

"Since we have only the two bedrooms I shall sleep on a little bed I shall put up in Mutti's room tonight. But I think you and Paul will be cozy enough in here?"

Laurel gasped.

"What is the matter?" Helga asked in surprise.

Laurel tried to cover her embarrassment.

"I think you've made a mistake. Paul and I hardly know each other – "

Helga gave a laugh before apologizing. "Oh, I am so sorry. You must try to forgive me. I thought you and Paul were already good friends and possibly becoming engaged. I was so determined to be modern and broadminded."

An unappetizing thought struck Laurel.

"Does Paul often bring his girlfriends here?"

Helga was shocked. "Oh, no – on just one occasion when he came to visit me before going to America. And that girl was his fiancée – "

"Oh!" Laurel let out her breath as though she'd been stung.

Helga didn't notice. "After what you have told me, I shall make up a bed for Paul in the living-room. He is a man and must rough it."

"I really could stay at a hotel to save putting you to any inconvenience – "

"No – please stay. It's so nice for me to have a little company. I see people so rarely now that I have to care for Mutti."

"Very well. But I shall only stay the one night."

When Laurel appeared downstairs ten minutes later she was looking more like the girl Paul had met on the plane. Her white polyester dress – the only uncrushable thing she had brought with her in the haversack – went excellently with her radiant-colored hair and the paleness of her skin.

The appreciative look in Paul's eyes told her all she wanted to know. And she felt satisfied. She had dressed up as much for his benefit as for her visit to Hohengrünfeld.

Although incredibly simple-looking, the dress had been hand-picked by her at an internationally known couturier's and even purchased at wholesale price had cost a lot of money.

"Very fetching. But I think I prefer you in jeans," he remarked with a smile, unable to take his eyes off her. "You make me nervous. Who knows what I'll spill over *that*?"

She was feeling happy and far less apprehensive about finding her sister.

"I'd forgive you much more easily this time. This dress happens to be off the peg and washable."

"Never mind – I still think it will be safer to keep my distance."

She felt a pinprick of disappointment at his decision.

"You can quite easily catch a bus to Hohengrünfeld," Helga told them, coming in from the kitchen. "It will save the expense of a taxi. If you ask for it by name I am sure the driver will put you off at the right stop."

They said goodbye and made for the nearest *Hältstelle*.

5

The bus journey to Hohengrünfeld, which lay to the southwest of the city, took about twenty minutes. It was almost seven by the time they reached there.

Huge iron gates barred their entry. They looked around for a bell.

"Nothing here," Paul said with a shake of his head. "I suppose we'll just have to take the risk that there may be guard dogs about." He tested the gates. "At least they're unlocked."

Laurel stayed close to his side as they made their way along the wide, leafy tunnel of a drive. His talk about guard dogs had made her feel uneasy. But there was no need to fear as they saw nothing of any on their way.

Before they had gone far they came to a small lodge cottage.

"Do you think we ought to inquire here first?" Laurel suggested.

"Maybe it would be best."

Going ahead of her up the path, he knocked on the weathered door. No one answered immediately and he knocked again, this time more enthusiastically.

An elderly voice screeched back at him in an

old German country dialect. "All right – all right – hold your horses, I'm coming as quickly as these old legs will allow."

A moment or two later they heard the sound of a rusty bolt being drawn and the door creaked slowly open.

On the threshold, rocking on shaky legs, was the oldest woman Laurel had ever seen. Her snow-white hair stuck out in untidy wisps and she had more wrinkles than could be counted. She looked older, even, than Helga's bed-ridden mother.

"We're extremely sorry to bother you," Paul said courteously, "but we've come a long way to pay a visit on the owner of Hohengrünfeld. Can you tell us if he's at home, and if it's in order for us to go on up to the *Herrenhaus?*"

The old lady eyed them suspiciously. "What do you want to see Herr von Haagen about?"

"It's a personal matter," Laurel told her.

Her words made the old woman cackle. "So are most matters, my pretty little lark. But, whatever it is, I doubt if you'll get much sense from him this evening. He's spent most of the day doing the rounds in his wheelchair. I spied him from my window. He'll be worn out and dozing by now – "

Laurel had great difficulty in understanding her dialect. But she caught the word "dozing" and queried it.

The woman grinned toothlessly. "It's what we old folk call giving our minds a bit of a rest.

But, if truth were told, Herr von Haagen's got very little mind to rest these days. He's fading fast – poor old fellow – "

"Old – did you say?"

"How old?" asked Paul.

The woman thought. "Could be eighty-five – could be eighty-six. It gets more and more difficult to remember. Younger than me, anyway. I was parlor maid up at the big house when he was just a young man."

Laurel grew disappointed. "In that case, I don't think we need bother him."

"Don't be a wash-out," Paul scolded her in English. Then he gave her a spontaneous hug. "Cheer up – the old girl's probably got it all wrong. Who's to say there's not a younger member of the von Haagen family? Since we've taken the trouble to come all the way here, I think we should carry on and inquire up at the house."

He took her hand firmly, leading her down the path and nodding their thanks to the old lady. Laurel regained her optimism, feeling comfort in the warmth of his clasp. Together they went on, following the curve of the drive until they reached the mansion.

Spying it first through the thick branches of its surrounding trees, Laurel thought what an awe-inspiring sight it presented. Hohengrünfeld was a magnificent building of gray stone with fine turrets. She judged it was probably about three centuries old, and lucky to have escaped the bombings in both wars.

Making their way up to the porticoed front door, Paul rang a huge brass bell that seemed to echo through the house like a roll of thunder.

He gave her a wink. "What's the betting we get Gagool's sister again?"

She smiled back, thinking how much he sometimes reminded her of Gavin. Yet he was far friendlier and far less arrogant.

Footsteps sounded from deep within, clickety-clacketing over a tiled surface and she pushed the thought away.

The door was opened by a pretty maidservant who stared at them in mild surprise as though few callers ever came.

"Can I help you?" she asked.

"We'd like to talk to Herr von Haagen," Paul told her.

She grew uncertain. "One moment, sir, and I'll find out if it's in order. Oh – er – would you like to come in and wait?"

They entered to find themselves in an ancestral hall, surrounded by suits of armor, colorful coats of arms and family portraits in huge, gilded frames.

"If you'll be good enough to wait in the sitting-room, I'll fetch Frau Nehls, the housekeeper."

The maidservant walked ahead of them, leading the way to a slightly less opulent room.

Laurel stared about her in slight distaste. All around the walls were mementoes of the hunt; boars' heads, deers' antlers, animal skins of all kinds, as well as spears and ancient rifles.

"I'd say Herr von Haagen was a blood-sports fan," Paul commented.

The maid left them there and tripped off again, her high-heeled shoes ringing across the polished tiles.

A few moments later, the housekeeper entered. She was middle-aged, gaunt and clothed in a no-nonsense dark suit. Her expression was sour.

Laurel instantly disliked her and left Paul to do the talking.

"Is it possible to have a word with Herr von Haagen?" he repeated.

"I'm afraid not," she said shortly. "Herr von Haagen has had a very busy day and he is getting ready to retire for the night."

Paul caught sight of Laurel's disappointment.

"Then I wonder if there's another member of the family we can talk to?"

"I'm sorry. But Herr von Haagen is the only surviving member of his family. There is no one else living here but he and his servants."

Laurel hid her despondency and brought out the newspaper cutting.

Struggling in slow German, she asked – "Then I wonder if you could tell me, please, how this photograph of Hohengrünfeld came to be in the paper? It's very important."

Frau Nehls took it and gave it a quick glance before dissmissing it with pouting lips.

"It looks like the one a reporter came to take some weeks ago. He paid me a small sum of money." She shrugged. "That's all I can tell you. And now I must ask you to leave."

"Oh, please wait – " the cry was torn from Laurel's heart. She knew that if she didn't make one last stand she would never forgive herself. "Surely there's someone else who can help us? You see, I'm trying to locate my sister. I'm sure there's some connection between this house and her disappearance. Can you tell me if there's anyone living here with the Christian name of Erich?"

"Of course – that happens to be my master's name. But I can assure you he has no interest in young ladies. If you must know, he happens to be in his eighties."

Laurel pleaded with her. "Are you sure there's no one else of that name – a footman – or a secretary -?"

The housekeeper lost patience.

"There is no one else of that name living here," she snapped.

Paul put his arm around Laurel's shoulder.

"Come on," he said gently, "I think we've exhausted this lead. Let's go back to Helga's."

She gave in with a despairing sigh. "You're right, of course. I was a fool to come all this way on a wild-goose chase. I must be going mental."

Frau Nehls led them out, her stern and unbending manner daring them to remain longer.

As they followed, for some unconscious reason, Laurel found herself examining the portraits. It was as they passed the most recent that she grabbed Paul by the sleeve.

"Look – look – tell me I'm dreaming, but I swear that's the man in my sister's photograph."

He followed her gaze, giving a whistle. "Good Lord, Laurel – I think you're right."

Frau Nehls was almost at the front door, she glared back in annoyance when she saw they'd stopped. But they ignored her.

"Have you got the snap with you?" he asked Laurel.

She shook her head, furious with herself. "No – I left it at Helga's when I changed."

"What's the matter – why have you stopped?" Frau Nehls wanted to know.

Paul beckoned to her. "One minute, please. This portrait – can you tell us who it's meant to be?"

She returned reluctantly.

"Why – it's Erich von Haagen, of course."

"There," Laurel cried, "I knew I was right."

"But I've already told you he's a very old man," the woman pointed out angrily. "That portrait was painted fifty years ago. Look at the date beneath if you don't believe me."

Laurel's gaze dropped to the writing beneath in German italics. The housekeeper was telling the truth. The date was 1937.

"But there must be some mistake," Laurel said with sinking heart. "How else can you account for the fact that I have a photo of this man with my sister?"

"If you do not leave this minute, I shall have no option but to send for the police," Frau Nehls told them.

"I really think we'd better do as she says," Paul told Laurel diplomatically. "We'll discuss this on our way back. Whatever the explanation to the riddle, we won't solve it by getting on the wrong side of people."

Laurel allowed him to lead her away from the house without making any more fuss, purely because there seemed nothing more she could do. Though, deep in her heart, she longed to be able to search the house from top to bottom to see if there was someone else living there. But it would have been pointless to refuse to go and be ignominiously ousted by the police.

As they passed the lodge cottage, both of them feeling frustrated and miserable, the old woman shouted out to them from her doorway.

"Well – what did I tell you? You didn't get any sense out of Erich von Haagen – I'll bet."

She gave a cackle of enjoyment. "And I doubt if you got any from that jumped-up housekeeper of his, either."

Laurel's spirits suddenly rose. She made Paul stop.

"Didn't that old woman say she used to be parlor maid there when von Haagen was a young man?"

He read her thoughts at once. "If you're thinking what I'm thinking – there's no harm in finding out all she knows."

They made for the lodge door.

It was some time later, over several cups of strong black coffee, and large glasses of schnapps for Paul and the old lady, that they finally came up with an answer to the puzzle.

Paul had made the old lady's eyes light up with the handful of notes he brought out of his wallet and placed in his coat pocket.

At his request for some information, she had led them into her parlor without more ado.

While Paul gleaned what he could, Laurel tried to follow the dialect. After her second schnapps the old woman was boasting importantly –

"Not many people know about that divorce except me – "

It was a word Laurel understood.

"What divorce?" she asked.

Paul gave a small shake of his head, reprimanding her.

"Hush, not now – it's taken two glasses of fire-water and irrevocable damage to my digestive system to get as far as this. I'll fill you in on everything later."

He turned to the old woman again. "Do go on with what you were telling us about the von Haagen household, ma'am."

Her old voice croaked on –

"– as I was saying, when the present von Haagen was a young man he married a woman from the south – Switzerland it was – let me see, the name was Camathias, if I remember – Theresa Camathias."

The woman cackled and slurped more schnapps.

"She was a pretty little thing. Far too sparkly and vivacious for such a serious man as Erich. Their marriage didn't stand a chance even from the beginning – though it was covered up well."

She cackled again and shook her head.

"But – they couldn't cover up all their arguments from us servants. We knew everything that went on in that *Herrenhaus,* all right. You can hide secrets from outsiders, but not from staff. Many's the time that young Swiss miss would scoot back to her mother – "

She went silent. Paul waved a note above her head and she went on again like clockwork.

"What was I saying – oh, yes – there was this divorce – or separation it might have been. They didn't approve of divorce among the hierarchy in those days like they do now. After it, little miss Fairyfeet took off for her homeland – somewhere near Konstanz it was – for about the tenth time." She gave a broad wink and tapped her nose with a gnarled finger. "This time she didn't go empty-handed. The high and mighty Erich made her take her baby son with her – didn't want to see it any more. Swore it wasn't his – "

"Son, did you say?" Paul said with more interest. "Now – do tell us more. I can see you've struck the jackpot, old mother. This all sounds extremely interesting – "

6

It was late by the time they left the lodge, so Paul and Laurel took a taxi back to Helga's. It was there they put her in the picture about all they had learned.

"A son!" she exclaimed. "But how exciting. That means he may be the man in the photograph with Laurel's sister."

Paul shook his head. "I doubt it. He'd be all of sixty if he's still alive. The separation took place well before the last war."

She looked crestfallen. "Then what good has your evening's work done?"

"We've still to find out. There's a chance Jenny's boyfriend could be the present von Haagen's grandson. His age and that of the man in the photo would be a lot closer, and resemblances often come out quite startlingly in the third generation."

"Then that likeness would prove von Haagen quite wrong when he accused his wife of having a child by another man." Helga paused. "What will you do now? Switzerland is hardly so small. How will you go about tracing such a person?"

"The family name is Camathias. And we've

even got an area – somewhere near Lake Constance."

Helga gave a satisfied nod. "You're very lucky. The old lodgekeeper was certainly no fool, in spite of her years. You seem to have plenty to go on."

She caught sight of Laurel, who had been silent all this while, trying to stifle a yawn.

"Oh, but look how selfish I am being keeping you both up. And your friend is so tired." She looked at her watch. "It's almost two. I must get sheets and blankets for you, Paul."

She was almost at the door of the living-room when she gave a laugh. "You know, I made such a stupid mistake when I was showing Laurel where she was to sleep. I presumed you would be sharing the same room. I didn't realize you had known each other such a short while. And there I was thinking I was being so modern."

As she left the room, Paul noticed the color that had flooded into Laurel's cheeks.

He teased her. "And what's so embarrassing about sharing a room with me? If you're afraid I snore – well, I don't."

She tossed her head. "It makes no difference to me whether you do or not – since there'll never be the chance to prove it either way."

She watched his blue eyes narrow, offering her a seductive challenge.

"Don't be so damned sure, Ruby Redhead. Stranger things have happened."

A silence descended between them that was almost tangible. Foolishly she felt her heart-beats quicken. To disguise what she was feeling she shook her head vehemently.

"Never! I have to feel something for a person before I sleep with them."

"And can you honestly say you feel nothing for me?"

Her limbs trembled. "The trouble with you, Paul Troughton, is that you drink too much."

His laughter followed her as she left the room and hurried up the stairs after Helga.

The next morning Paul's kind German friend gave them a train time-table to study while she prepared breakfast.

"There's a train that leaves in an hour," Paul said. "If we catch it, we should arrive at Constance about one. How does that sound?"

Laurel, who had spoken little since she'd come downstairs, gave a short nod. She was still wondering how she could tell him she no longer wanted him to help her. It would be embarrassing to do it there at Helga's. Maybe she should wait until they were on their way to the station.

He stroked his chin thoughtfully, studying her. "What's up? Didn't *you* sleep well, either?"

"I'm perfectly all right," she assured him quickly. "I'll just help Helga bring in the breakfast things."

As she passed him he caught her wrist, pulling her back.

"I asked you what was wrong, Laurel. I've known you long enough to tell when something's up. Answer me – what have I done wrong?"

She snatched her wrist away, her hazel eyes flashing fire.

"That's just it, Paul Troughton. You don't know me at all. And I don't know you. We met on a train. I think we should call it a day and each go our separate ways from now on."

He stared down at her angry, upturned countenance.

Then he gave a shrug. "Very well, if that's what you want."

"And I do!"

He gave a lazy smile. "I don't suppose you'll have any objection if I accompany you as far as the station. After all – the railroad's open to all."

"No – I've no objection," she said softly, leaving the room.

On the way to the station they spoke little. Then Laurel asked him a question that, among others, had been bothering her most of the night.

"Helga mentioned you were engaged to be married. Do you and your fiancée usually take separate vacations?"

He was quiet before he replied. And his voice was unusually serious.

"There's no fiancée any more, Laurel. She died some months ago and I'm still having a hard time getting over it."

"Oh – I'm sorry – I had no idea – I thought – "

He gave a bitter laugh.

"Oh, yes, I can guess what you thought. Man on loose makes up to damsel in distress while his affianced sweetheart remains at home sewing up her trousseau – "

"I thought nothing of the sort. I just wondered what had happened to her."

"Well, now you know." For the first time since she'd known him his voice was angry. "Anyway – what about you? I haven't noticed any ring, but I doubt if you're as footloose and fancy-free as you appear. Is there anyone special knocking about at home worrying himself sick over your escapade?"

She didn't really want to talk about Gavin and how badly she'd been let down. But, now that he'd told her about his fiancée, she felt bound to.

"There *was* someone – a month or so ago – but we agreed to part because we weren't suited. Or, to be more accurate – it appeared *I* didn't suit him."

She felt him studying her.

"I find that very difficult to believe."

"And why's that?" she asked sharply.

They were making their way toward the busy station approach. He stopped in his tracks and stared down at her.

"Only because I think anyone who was fortunate enough to become engaged to you would be a head case to let you go."

She stared back, rounding her full lips in a taut "oh." For a long moment they stared at each other. Then he broke the spell.

"Don't look at me like that, Laurel. You've no idea what it does to me."

She turned away, allowing the thrill of pleasure at his foolhardy words to engulf her.

Then she pulled herself up with a jerk. This was madness to experience these feelings for someone she hardly knew. As she'd told him, they were virtually strangers. They'd met on a plane, a bus and a train. And yet she felt she knew him better than she knew a lot of people.

"You'd better hurry if you don't want to miss your train," he reminded her.

"What train?" she asked frowning.

He gave a laugh. "The one you're catching to Constance – alone. Or had you forgotten?" He glanced at his watch. "You've got exactly seven minutes to find the booking office and purchase a ticket–" he broke off. "What's the matter? You've gone as white as a sheet. Don't try to flatter me my company means *that* much to you – "

"That man?" she pointed, wide-eyed with fear.

He tried to follow her line of vision.

"Which one?" People were coming and going briskly all around.

"The one waiting outside the station – "

"Turned up collar and trilby hat?"

She nodded, swallowing hard before trying to explain.

"I met him in Cologne. He had a knife. He was going to stab me. I thought he'd mistaken me for someone else. But he's followed me here."

"In that case – quick!" He took her sleeve, dragging her over to where people were boarding a motor coach. "With a bit of luck we'll lose him. I doubt if he's seen you yet."

"But I'll miss that train."

"Too bad. You can catch another. A few hours won't make any difference."

They joined the end of the queue. Laurel tried to hide the striking color of her hair by pulling Jenny's bobble-hat on again. Paul asked the man in front the coach's destination.

"Horb am Neckar," he was told.

Paul gave a shrug. "I can't say I know it. Hopefully it's in the same direction as Constance."

A moment later they had boarded and paid their fares. He stowed their haversacks on the rack above before settling down beside her.

"I should keep your head well down," he told her. "Old Bluebeard'll have a tough job to recognize you from that distance. But you don't want to take any chances. In fact, I've a better idea – if I put my arm around you like this, and you tuck your head into my shoulder, he'll have difficulty distinguishing you at all."

As he wrapped her in his arm, she caught a whiff of his after-shave. The sensation of being so close to him was heady and exhilarating as well as being warm and comforting.

A few moments later the coach left. Reluctantly she pulled away from him.

"There's no need to do that unless you really want to," he said softly.

She realized that they were still together, when they'd arranged to part at the station.

"Yes, I really want to," she said tightly. "And please Paul, don't read anything more into what just happened than there really is. I allowed you to put your arm around me simply so that I could leave Stuttgart safely without that terrible man seeing me – "

He listened to her in silent disbelief before giving a burst of laughter.

"Now who's telling fibs? You don't seriously expect me to believe all that stuff you told me about a man with a knife, do you?"

She exploded. "It's the truth."

"Oh, yes – I forgot. It's 'fool old Paul day,' isn't it? And now it's time to bring on Jack the Ripper. Who else have we saved for later – Frankenstein?"

He ignored her look of fury.

"Are you sure that everything else you've

told me about having a missing sister isn't a pack of lies, too? You're not really some kind of nut who makes up dramas about herself, are you?"

She turned her face angrily to the window.

"Don't talk to me any more, please. And when this bus stops, will you please get out of my life and stop pestering me with your unwanted advances – "

"Pull the other one. I'm beginning to wonder if you've escaped from a funny farm. In fact – just a minute – are you sure you haven't been pulling the wool over my eyes all along with that trumped-up photo of a so-called sister?" He frowned pensively. "I doubt if you even have a twin. That snap could just as easily be of you – with some guy who resembles old von Haagen." He shook his head at her. "Is that the way you get your kicks – from trying to fool poor, innocent travelers like me?"

Laurel could hardly believe her ears. How dare he accuse her of making everything up? For once in her life she kept her temper sternly under control, speaking with dignity.

"You're perfectly entitled to believe whatever you wish. And now let's get one thing straight. In spite of my wishes, you've had the audacity to go on following me around when I've made my wishes quite clear in that respect. I want you to understand that when we reach this Horb am Neckar place, I don't want to see you any more. As far as I'm concerned you've never existed. Can I have your assurance on that?"

He took her hand solemnly.

"Indeed you have. And have I your assurance that you won't pull any more fast ones in order to retain my services?"

She blushed just as fiercely as if she'd been really guilty of it.

"Don't utter another word to me." She stood up in the speeding bus. "And kindly let me pass. I'll spend the rest of the journey in that empty seat over there."

When they finally arrived at Horb am Neckar Laurel made sure she got off ahead of Paul. At once she set off in search of the railroad station. Looking behind just before she reached it, she was relieved, but, at the same time, slightly disappointed to see him nowhere in sight.

Well, she told herself briskly, that was precisely what she wanted, wasn't it? She had told him she no longer wished to have anything to do with him and thank goodness, he had taken her at her word. So it was good riddance to bad rubbish?

All the same, she couldn't get rid of a peculiar sense of loss.

At the station she found she had taken a good percentage off her journey to Constance by catching the coach, and that the city lay only about three hours journey away.

The next train was due in an hour's time.

She would have to change at Singen. But, with luck, she would still arrive at her destination in plenty of time to find a room in a small hotel for the night.

Tomorrow she would start her quest for Jenny in earnest, armed with everything Paul had managed to glean from the old lady at the lodge.

The thought pricked her conscience. It had been all through his excellent linguistic ability that they had discovered so much. About the fact that Erich von Haagen had an estranged wife and son in Switzerland. On her own, she could never have managed to understand what the old lady, with her country dialect, was talking about. She also owed him the money he had paid for the information.

The thought appalled her, especially when she recalled that she had also spent the night for nothing at his friend's house. In fact, if it hadn't been for him, she might have had to spend it in some small, unfriendly hotel with a landlady like Frau Lindt.

In fact, the more she thought about it, he had been a tower of strength in almost every way. And now, foolishly, she was missing him. Missing him badly – and not just for all his kindness in helping her. But for some other reason. A reason she found difficulty putting into words.

What was this curious thing she felt for him?

Surely it couldn't be more than a slight infatuation that she'd soon get over? Or could it?

7

Laurel's journey to Constance by train was superb, speeding through the Black Forest with thick pines on either side. Now and then she caught sight of snippets of English countryside with surprisingly rolling downs. Then the train sped out of these scenes and away through the forest again as though the open vistas had been just a mirage.

They passed through small towns, each with their dozens of window boxes filled with sprawling geraniums. The afternoon sun shone down on out-of-town allotments that were all aglow with summer flowers.

But Laurel's mind took in none of the scenic splendor. All she could think of was Paul – wondering whether he had gone back to Stuttgart and Helga – or whether he'd taken another motor coach to somewhere else.

But what did any of that matter, anyway, she asked herself with a sigh? They had been merely strangers, passing in the night. She would never see him again – and, what was more, they had parted in anger. That thought made her infinitely sad.

When she finally arrived at Constance station

the first thing she did was to stow her haversack into a locker in the Left Luggage department while she searched for somewhere to stay. She had already decided that it would be best to find a hotel in the immediate vicinity so that she wouldn't have so far to return to the station in the morning once she started her quest in earnest.

But every hotelier she tried told her they were full. Or maybe they were put off by the sight of her in scruffy old jeans, she thought.

It wasn't until evening started to fold in that she decided she would have to search for somewhere to stay further away from the city center.

Returning wearily to the station she collected her haversack once more. And, just outside, she met a group of laughing English hikers, dressed in jeans and jumpers like herself.

"It's no good trying to find a hotel in the city," she told them in a friendly way. "I've just tried and they don't have any vacancies at all."

The girl nearest gave a laugh. "I wouldn't dream of it," she replied in a London accent. "Much too pricy. If I could have afforded to come on *that* sort of holiday I wouldn't be loaded down like a packhorse, the way I am now."

"Then where will you stay?" Laurel asked.

"At a Youth Hostel, I hope."

"Are there such things around here?"

"You must be joking. I tell you what – if

you're really serious, tag along with us. Rick's been to Constance before. He knows just where it is."

"Thanks." Laurel gave a smile of relief. It was nice to feel she was no longer alone. It was good to be with a crowd of other English – although they were probably years younger than her and only in their teens.

The Youth Hostel lay a bus ride away, several miles out of the city. Rick, who was in his last year at school in England, told her it was a Water Tower, with the water above and the Youth Hostel below.

Once they alighted from the bus the six of them walked in single file along a narrow path through a field of ripening maize. A full moon had come out, turning the Water Tower into a dark silhouette against a background of distant mountains.

When they arrived at the well-appointed hostel, Laurel left Rick to do most of the talking while she waited with the rest of the party. It was only when the man behind the reception desk asked for her Hosteling card that she looked blank.

"Don't you have one?" Rick asked sympathetically. "That's tough. They've generally only room here for genuine hostelers. I doubt if you'll be allowed to stay without your card."

The receptionist gave an abrupt shake of his head. He replied in English with a German accent.

"That's perfectly true. I am afraid I cannot enrol you here. We are expecting a party of seventy schoolchildren this evening. As your friend says, I can only take genuine hostelers."

"What will you do?" the girl Laurel had first spoken to outside the station asked with a worried look.

"I've no idea," Laurel told her brusquely. "But it's quite obvious I'm not wanted here. Don't lose any sleep over me – I shall be quite all right. I'll probably just have to sleep rough, that's all."

"But aren't you afraid of rapists?"

Laurel gave her what she hoped was a withering look. If it hadn't been for her airy invitation to "tag along" with them in the first place, it was possible she might have found a guest-house to stay in by now. As it was, finding her way back to Constance was going to be difficult. She had no idea which way they'd come, for one thing.

She said goodbye and left the bright lights of reception behind. Once outside, she tried to recall from which direction they'd arrived. There seemed to be fields of maize all over the place.

A quarter of an hour later, still with no more idea of her whereabouts, she was standing, looking lost in the center of one of the fields, when a voice close at hand began to intone, in a voice that warmed her heart –

"– and there was this poor little red-headed

waif, whom nobody wanted, turned out into the snow with nowhere to go – "

She turned quickly and gladly to see Paul, standing on the other side of a row of maize, looking over at her with an amused grin on his good-looking face.

But, much as his unexpected presence gladdened her heart, she had no intention of letting him know that.

"Oh, not *you* again. I thought I had enough problems on my plate without you adding to them."

"Spoken like a woman. In that case, I'll take myself off."

The moon disappeared suddenly behind a cloud and he seemed to vanish as though he'd been merely a figment of her wishful imagination.

"Oh, Paul – I didn't mean it. Where are you?"

The moon came out again and she saw he was still there. He hadn't moved an inch.

"At your command, ma'am," he said with a mock bow.

"How did you get here, anyway?" she asked. "You haven't, by any chance, been following me about without my knowledge – probably having a good laugh?"

"Now – would I do that?"

"Of course you would. In fact, I suspect you of having quite a sadistic nature."

"Well, if you must know," he informed her.

"I was fortunate enough to catch another coach almost straight away that arrived in Constance an hour before your train from Singen. So, I got myself a room and then hung about at the station waiting for you – "

"You beast!"

He laughed. "As you've discovered, I have this sadistic streak. I wanted to find out how you'd really get on – on your own – without my help. And you didn't get very far, did you?"

She looked away, feeling tears of gratitude for his unexpected presence well up in her eyes.

"No," she said in a small voice.

"Well, come on, then. It's late and I could do with a meal. Have you eaten at all since we parted?"

She shook her head.

"Neither have I. Do you realize I've been losing weight steadily ever since I met you? I shall probably get back to England a shadow of my former self. And that will be all your fault."

"I'm sorry."

"So you jolly well should be. Here – pass me your haversack and take my hand. I don't want to have to bail you out of a police cell, when some irate German farmer has you booked for breaking down his crop."

It was heaven to feel his closeness again. She hadn't realized meeting him once more would be as incredibly wonderful as this.

Together they found a track that led steeply down to the edge of the lake. Coming out by the side of a brewery, they went through a disused garden and emerged by a cafe.

"I think this will do," Paul told her. "It's not a very pretty sight but I guess we're both too hungry to notice."

Laurel wasn't feeling all that hungry. She was too delighted just being with him again to think about food.

But, when an appetizing meal was placed in front of her by a friendly *Frau* in an ample overall, she found she could do justice to it.

After they'd finished, she asked him – "Where did you say this room of yours was?"

"Back in the city."

"And do you think they'll have another room for me?"

He studied her face pensively from just above the rim of his coffee cup, making her heart turn over as she gazed into the fascinating blue of his eyes.

"I'm not all that sure. Will it matter very much if they don't? You'd have a chance to learn whether I snore or not, after all."

"I couldn't possibly do that, Paul."

"Why not?"

"You know why not."

"Because we hardly know each other?"

"That – among other things."

"Like what?"

"Oh, don't be so persistent. You know perfectly well."

"How can I – if you won't put things into words?"

"Don't let's discuss it any more," she said.

"Very well."

Paul paid for their meal and they left. Soon after, they found a bus stop and caught a bus back to the city. A little while later she walked through the door of his hotel with him.

"We'd like another room," he said to the desk clerk.

The man looked from one to the other. "You mean a double one instead of the single you already have?"

"No – I mean two single rooms," Paul told him.

The man examined the register before shaking his head.

"I'm sorry, sir, that is impossible. All our accommodation had been booked heavily because of an exhibition that is opening in Konstanz tomorrow." He studied the register again. "The only thing I can do is perhaps change your room for a double." He looked at Laurel before giving a discreet smile. "I should think your answer would depend on how well you know each other. I would hasten to add that the room has separate sleeping accommodation in that it contains two beds."

Laurel shook her head emphatically. "No,

that's quite impossible. We're not sharing the same room."

The desk clerk gave a shrug. "Then I am afraid there is no other way I can help. I would advise you that you may find great difficulty obtaining a room anywhere else in view of what I have told you – " he gave a glance at a nearby clock – "and in view of the late hour."

"Can you give us a moment to discuss this?"

"Naturally, sir."

Paul led her into a corner of the large reception hall. Then he looked down at her, his expression considerate but intense.

"Don't let me influence you in any way, Laurel. I'm perfectly willing to let you have my room and I'll sleep on a bench on the station – "

"Don't be ridiculous! All you're doing is twisting my arm," she whispered fiercely. "You know I can't possibly allow you to do that."

"Well, there's only the other alternative, and you've made your feelings pretty clear on that."

She looked out at the dark night, furious with the way the situation had worked out. Why had fate brought them together only to land her with such a difficult decision to make? She wasn't ready to start another affair so soon after her let-down over Gavin. For one thing she wasn't really certain that what she felt for Paul was not just infatuation. They'd only known each other a few days. And now she was being thrown in at the deep end where their relationship was concerned.

"If it's any consolation to you," he promised softly, "you have my word that there'll be no funny business on my part. Much as you attract me, I've never been known to force my attentions where they may not be reciprocated. There'll be you in your single bed, and I in mine. And never the twain shall meet – except, perhaps, where washing or changing facilities are concerned. But I'm quite sure there'll be a separate bathroom along the corridor that one of us can use."

At that moment the reception clerk beckoned to him. They went over together.

"I just thought I'd reassure you, sir and madam, that I have telephoned to the other gentleman who has the double room, and he is quite willing to exchange with you for your single room – if that is what you require."

Paul gave her a quick, interrogative look. "What do you say?"

It was now or never, she decided, before she got cold feet. But it was the most difficult decision that had ever been wrenched from her. Still, provided Paul kept his word, what actual harm could it do? No one else would ever find out. The secret of how she'd shared a room with a virtual stranger would be theirs alone.

She gave a reluctant nod of her head. "Very well."

"Good girl." He gave her an understanding smile.

The porter showed them up half an hour later, after the reception clerk had made sure the rooms had been vacated satisfactorily.

Laurel felt her excitement and apprehension rise as the door closed behind them and they were left alone. The room was pretty, almost feminine. And it had a pronounced character – hardly what she would have expected from a commercial hotel.

Paul placed her haversack on the end of one of the beds.

"Which one would you like? Personally, I'm easy. I've slept in so many hotel rooms since I left England for the States that I found in the end I could sleep facing north, south, east or west – " he broke off. "But you may have a distinct preference?"

"No – I've none at all," she murmured, trying to hide her embarrassment. "I'll sleep in the bed nearest the door, if you like."

"So that you can make a speedy get-away if I break my promise? I can assure you that won't be necessary."

"I didn't mean that, at all," she said quickly.

Hiding her expression, she burrowed through her haversack to find her washing tackle and night things.

"I'll see if there's a bathroom somewhere," she informed him, leaving the room.

"I'll make sure the door is on the latch for you," he called after her. "I'll probably be in bed when you get back."

With her face half hidden by the duvet, Laurel gazed out at the stars. They had both agreed that they preferred to sleep with the drapes undrawn and the window partly open.

She lay thinking over the events of the day, marveling at the way Paul had caught the coach, then waited around for her train to arrive so that he could follow her and keep a watchful eye on her, in spite of their bitter argument and the angry words they'd exchanged. It must mean he felt something more than just a fleeting sexual attraction for her, didn't it? But what?

She realized they hadn't discussed their argument since and wondered if he still felt the same.

"Are you still awake?" she whispered.

"Uh-uh!"

"Did you really mean it when you accused me of telling lies about the man I saw at the station?"

"I don't know. Tell me about it again."

"You already know. That person was the same one who threatened me with a knife in Cologne. He made a promise at the time that I hadn't seen the last of him."

"Is that the honest truth?"

"Of course it's the truth. You didn't really think I'd make up anything so stupid, just so you could drag me onto that coach and we'd be together?"

"I rather hoped so."

"Well, you can take that satisfied smirk off your face, Paul Troughton. Because I can assure you it *was* the truth."

"How did you know I was smirking?"

"I guessed. It's the sort of thing you do."

"Is that the kind of opinion you have of me, Laurel?"

His voice, pitched low, made her give an involuntary shiver. She would have loved to turn over, just to catch sight of him in the dark. It was amazing what he could do to her just by altering his tone.

"Go to sleep," she whispered hoarsely.

There was silence for a few seconds before he broke it, speaking in hard-done-by accents.

"I said I wouldn't thrust my attentions on you unless you wanted me to. But I didn't promise to sleep. I don't know how the hell you expect me to, knowing you're only inches away."

Her reply was muffled. "You'll just have to try to think about something else. Why don't you take an aspirin–?"

The laugh he gave threatened to wake up everyone else on their floor.

"Don't make that noise," she said angrily. "People will wonder what we're doing."

He exploded with mirth again. "If people knew the true situation, which they couldn't possibly, they'd be extremely disappointed, wouldn't they?"

"Don't talk. I'm tired and I want to go to sleep," she lied.

"Oh – I'm extremely sorry," he retorted sarcastically. "But, if I remember rightly, it was *you* opened this conversation. I thought, when you switched off your light and said goodnight, that it would be the last I'd hear of you till morning." His voice dropped. "Don't test me too much, Laurel. I'm only human, after all."

"You made a promise," she reminded him.

"Yes – and I can just as easily break it. I don't think I mentioned that I was frequently caned for lying when I was a child – "

"Oh, be quiet!"

8

"Do you take milk with your coffee – I'm afraid I don't remember?" Laurel asked.

Paul gazed at her across the breakfast table, marveling at how wide-awake and beautiful she looked, in spite of their lack of sleep.

"I take coffee black – no sugar – no milk. You really ought to get used to that if we're going to make what happened last night a regular habit – "

"Well, we're not," she said lightly. "It's the first and last time I've ever shared a room with someone I've known such a short time. And I certainly shan't be making a habit of it."

He smiled lopsidedly at her, one side of his mouth turning down at the corner in the heart-warming way it had of stirring her emotions.

"I guess last night stops us being strangers any more," he murmured.

She shook her head. "And there you're quite wrong. I knew my fiancé, Gavin, for two months before we even so much as kissed – "

He interrupted. "And I knew Fern for just five minutes – "

She looked at him in surprise. "Who's Fern?"

"*My* fiancée – the girl I told you about who died – "

"Oh, yes – of course."

His mention of his dead fiancée built a barrier between them. Laurel felt envious. In a masochistic way, she wanted to learn everything about her. At the same time, she dreaded his answer to her next question.

She posed it softly. "Do you think you'll ever get over her?"

He looked into the distance toward the mountains sheathed in mist that they could see through the French windows of the hotel breakfast room.

"There are times when I feel I have. Times like last night." He threw her a glance. "You might as well know that when I was in the States I tried sleeping with other girls just to get the perfume of her body out of my mind. But it never worked. She was always there, between the other girl and me. It was just as though, even in death, she was defying me to find anyone else so irresistibly lovely – "

His talk increased the jealousy Laurel was feeling so much that she gave a pointed look at her watch.

"I'm sorry to cut your reminiscences short but we haven't yet discussed where we're going to start on our quest to find my sister." She paused. "I presume you still want to help me. That's surely the reason you followed me to Constance?"

He looked back at her measuredly, as though seeing her for the first time.

"No, Laurel," he said quietly – "believe it or not – that wasn't the reason – " he broke off. "But we won't go into that right now."

Reaching into his pocket he pulled out a map of Switzerland.

"I went to the kiosk outside and bought this while you were showering. Since that old woman said the Camathias family had a large house somewhere near the lake, I thought we'd do the thing systematically." He stretched the map across the table. "If we cover this area inch by inch, it shouldn't take too long to visit all the towns and villages on the Swiss side of the lake, to find out if anyone of the name of Camathias still lives thereabouts."

He paused. "Oh, yes – I also dropped into an office nearby and saw someone about hiring a car. I've already filled in the papers. They promised to leave it outside the hotel for us – "

She stared at him. What he was telling her heightened her respect for him. But her pride wouldn't let her show it. He had as good as told her he would never get over his fiancée. Even if she allowed herself to admit she was in love with him, what was the good of harboring any fancy thoughts about their future relationship?

"That's extremely kind and business-like of you," she murmured gratefully. "I hadn't even got as far as organizing a car. I suppose I might, eventually. But you seem to have put everything into action so quickly."

"Praise from Laurel Brownridge is praise indeed," he teased her. "But don't commend me on how quick I've been. Believe me, I had plenty of time. You're forgetting how long you spend in a bathroom."

She drew back her chair. "All the more reason to make up for that now. If you've finished your coffee shall we get started?"

"Not only proud, but a slave-driver as well," he muttered.

She hesitated as they made their way toward the hall. "Oh – one thing about last night – " she broke off, trying to find the right words.

"Yes?" he asked expectantly.

She looked up at him. "I insist on you letting me pay my share of the bill. And I also want to pay for the car hire and the purchase of that map – oh, yes – and the amount you gave that old lady for the information – "

His eyes narrowed as he glared down at her. "And how about the coach fare – you forgot about that?"

"Oh, yes – I'm sorry."

"And while we're about it," he went on in murderous tones – "we might as well add in my plane fare from England, the bus ride I took in Cologne and my train fare to Stuttgart – "

"I – I don't think that's really very fair."

"Oh, come on," he said, taking her firmly by the arm. "Go up and get your things – and if you so much as mention payment to me again our association will be at an end. I shall clear out and leave you to your own devices." His tone became scathing. "And we both know how inept you are in difficult situations."

She left him at the reception desk and ran up the stairs, feeling like a small child who'd been sent up to her room in disgrace.

For the most part of the next few days they drew a blank in every town and village they came to. It was only when evening began to draw in on the third day of their search around the lake that they had their first real piece of good fortune.

The hired car had developed a fault in one of the brakes which had grown steadily worse. Paul drew up at a garage to see if they could fix it for him.

It was as they drove to a standstill that Laurel glimpsed the name they were seeking. It was staring at them from a small signpost. If they'd gone driving past the garage at speed they would probably have missed it.

"Paul – look there! CAMATHIAS! It's the name we've been asking everyone about. Do you think there can be a connection? Would people actually name a village after a family?"

"If the family were noble or important enough. It's possible a village even grew up around the Camathias household."

Before they were able to follow up the important lead, Paul spoke to the garage mechanic, who was preparing to go off duty.

"We've a fault in the front offside brake. Do you think there's a chance you could fix it for us?"

The man gave a glance at his watch. Laurel crossed her fingers.

"It's possible," he said.

"If you could, I'd be extremely grateful," Paul told him.

To their delight the fault took less than half an hour to put right. Paul tipped the mechanic generously, and they were on their way again.

The country road they veered on to, took them directly down to the lake. It glowed and shimmered in the moonlight, every ripple illuminated by the lights of river boats that crossed and recrossed its wide expanse.

Laurel called out excitedly as she caught sight of high iron gates through a gap in the hedge as they turned the next bend in the narrow road.

"That could be it!"

Paul stopped the car in front of them.

"I can't see a name," he said, giving a shake of his head.

Laurel got out.

"Oh, but there is," she told him, pointing the light of their torch at the stonework.

Etched deeply into the ancient gateposts, partially obliterated by the passage of time, was the single name – CAMATHIAS

Paul followed her, giving her an affectionate squeeze as he reached her side.

"We've made it, Laurel. And it's all thanks to your sharp sight, happening to catch sight of that signpost by the garage." He gave a sigh. "Let's hope we're coming to the end of our search."

It was the closest they'd been for days – since they'd shared his room in Constance. Suddenly the warmth of his body sent an urgent longing inside her that made her forget the only reason they had come so far was to find her sister.

Her heart was beating as fast as she'd ever known it.

Paul seemed to feel it and looked down. He blamed the moonlight for bringing out a softened glow in her eyes that he'd never seen there before.

"Oh, Laurel, my darling – " he murmured.

She was incapable of replying. And even if she had, no power on earth would have made her forgo their first kiss.

Folding her tenderly in his arms, he bent his face to hers, discovering her moist, receptive lips. Her heart-beats rose to a breathless crescendo as he crushed his mouth to hers.

Moments later, she leant against his shoulder trembling.

"Don't ask me how that happened," he murmured. "I'm not capable of heavy thought at the moment."

He went on holding her, as though to let her

go would be the most foolish thing he'd ever done in his life.

And now I can never go back, she told herself. I can never go back to thinking Gavin the only person I shall ever love. This man in my arms belongs to me – even if it's only for this moment. Then a warning note struck in her breast.

Tread softly, my heart – for how can mortals tell what their uncertain futures will bring?

How long she remained in Paul's arms, she never knew. All she was aware of was the sweetness. Their embrace had happened so suddenly, after days of longing, that one moment they were overjoyed about finding the house, and the next she was locked in his arms, never wanting to be set free.

"Words should be left unsaid at times like these," Paul said softly, murmuring into her hair. "Do you know – I've wanted to kiss you almost from the first moment I set eyes on you – "

"Even when you spilt your drink all over me?" For the first time she was teasing *him*.

His answer was to kiss her again, this time with even more ardor, sending her senses reeling.

"Laurel, my sweet, every minute I'm with you I want you more and more," he said breathlessly. "But at no time in my life as much as I wanted you the other night."

"I want you, too."

A car drove by, pinning them in the headlamps. He released her reluctantly.

"Shall we take a rain check on this conversation? he smiled. "Much as I would love to go on holding you, there will be better places and better times. Let's finish the quest we started first."

For the only time in her life, Laurel wished she hadn't been born a twin. Then she threw the thought away, ashamed of herself. As Paul said, there would be other times. And this moment would never die in her heart. But they were here to find Jenny. If she'd never started her search she wouldn't have met Paul. So she could always be grateful to Jenny for bringing them together in such a roundabout way.

As they drove up the curving drive it reminded her a little of the time they'd gone to Hohengrünfeld. But, if the house in Stuttgart had been imposing, this was more so, In the moonlight it resembled a fairy castle – the lake and the mountains lending it an air of mystery that would probably be lost in daytime.

They drove to the bottom of the marble steps. As he led Laurel up them, he kissed her once more while they waited for their summons to be answered.

"I shall keep my fingers firmly crossed for you," he breathed.

When the door opened, Laurel knew at once, by the look of recognition on the woman's face, that they had found the right house.

"Oh, Miss Brownridge – none of us was expecting you back till tomorrow. Oh, but – " the Swiss housekeeper's face took in Paul in surprise – "but, my master?" The kindly face dropped. "I pray God nothing is wrong?"

Laurel shook her head. "I'm not the person you think I am. Jenny Brownridge is my twin sister. But I'm so pleased to hear you're expecting her."

A look of relief passed over the woman's face.

"Of course, Madam. I should have realized. Your sister told me about you. I do hope you received the letter she gave me to post two weeks ago."

Laurel stared at her in surprise. "A letter – no! I certainly never received one."

The housekeeper looked mystified. "But I posted it to you myself – or rather – " her face reddened – "I remember now, I gave it to the under-housemaid who was just going on holiday. She promised she'd post it from Konstanz."

"Well, I never received anything of the sort," Laurel said with a trace of annoyance. "And, what's more, I've been half out of my mind with worry. You've no idea what an arduous time we've had tracing her. And even now I'm not sure what she's doing here when I thought she was in Cologne."

The woman started wringing her hands. "Oh, merciful heaven, I shall never forgive myself. I should never have entrusted such an important letter to anyone else. But the household was all upset. And such a time for anyone to go on holiday with the master so ill – "

"It's no use crying over spilt milk," Laurel said with a shrug. "Since the letter's gone astray perhaps you'll tell us what made my sister give up her job and leave Germany to come here?"

Paul glanced about.

"I'm sure you have somewhere more comfortable than the hallway where we can discuss this?"

The housekeeper was mortified.

"Naturally, sir – madam. You must forgive me for being so confused. If you will follow me I will arrange for refreshments to be brought straight away to the sitting-room."

Later, over plentiful cups of coffee, Frau Bruder, who had been with the Camathias household for the last twenty years, put them in the picture.

9

Since Laurel's sister was expected back in the morning, Frau Bruder insisted on arranging for Laurel and Paul to stay there the night in the south wing, overlooking the lake.

In her room next door to Paul's, Laurel ached to be with him. But they had agreed by mutual consent to control their passion until they had had time to come to terms with the incredible thing that had happened to them.

"No names – no pack drill!" Paul pointed out. "How would one of us feel if we woke up to find that what we felt for the other was only infatuation, after all." He'd looked deeply at Laurel. "I couldn't bear that, and I know you couldn't either. We've both been through a lot of emotional torment, Laurel. Let's make sure we're not just making use of each other before we get too deeply in."

She had agreed, at the same time knowing that what she felt for him was truly love. But, as he had said, it would be heart-breaking for her to give herself to him, and then find out their relationship had no base but sex.

As she lay awake in the magnificent carved oak bed, feeling his burning kisses still on her lips, and listening to the sepulchral wail of a ship's siren on the lake, something like a lost soul in purgatory, she went over in her mind the story the housekeeper had told them. At times it had been so involved she'd had difficulty following it.

It seemed Jenny had left her position as nurse manager at the clinic in Cologne due to the illogical behavior of one of the psychiatric patients. The woman had developed a murderous dislike of her for no apparent reason. Since the patient was highly dangerous, it was thought better by all, especially the psychiatrist in charge of the patient, that Jenny should leave as soon as possible.

The decision was not as dire as it may have seemed, since, at the time, she was preparing to become engaged to one of the younger psychiatrists – Erich Camathias-Jundt – the owner of the house where Laurel was staying – and would shortly have been giving in her notice, anyway.

When Erich had brought her to Switzerland, they had told Frau Bruder they intended getting married in England sometime before Christmas. But their joy was all but destroyed when, soon after their arrival, Erich was involved in an accident. His spine was injured, and at first it was feared he would never walk again. But a friend of his, another doctor, had given them renewed hope.

For the past two weeks Jenny had been staying in Zurich, close to one of the best teaching hospitals in Switzerland. A week ago she had been in touch with Frau Bruder to let her know Erich's operation had been a great success, and that they would be coming home in seven days.

That time was up tomorrow. It was when Laurel would see her twin sister again. They would have so much to tell each other.

In spite of all that had happened, Laurel succeeded in falling asleep. But she awoke soon after dawn, her thoughts filled with love for the man sleeping next door.

How would she have reacted, she wondered, if she'd had to go through the same trauma as Jenny? Seeing the man she loved in such pain? No wonder she'd had no time to phone or explain. Her heart saddened. Perhaps, even at this moment, Jenny was thinking badly of her for not replying to that letter she'd never received. Well, all that would be swiftly sorted out the moment they met.

Laurel got up early. It was not quite six, but she decided to shower and dress and take the opportunity of exploring the grounds on her own. Her love for Paul was still so new that she needed solitude to come to terms with it.

Leaving silently by the front door, she skirted the house and found, to her delight, that the grounds of the magnificent mansion stretched right to the shores of the lake. Some time later, standing on the beach, watching a flock of wild ducks flying in formation across the mirror-like surface of Lake Constance, she looked back through the thick branches of walnut trees, thinking how fortunate Jenny was to be marrying someone who owned such a splendid place.

It was then she realized with a start how little she knew about Paul. She wasn't sure what he did for a living, only that he'd taken time off to go to the States. But she still didn't know what he'd been doing there.

What lay ahead of them, she wondered, smiling? Even if he ever got as far as asking her to marry him, where would they live? In her apartment? In lodgings he might have? With a touch of uncertainty, she wondered if he would expect her to sell out her partnership in Laureder's.

She made a face at herself as she thought of what Derrick would say when she told him she'd fallen in love with a stranger who seemed to have appointed himself her guardian angel ever since she left the shores of England.

Then, coming out of her reverie, she gave a glance at her watch to find it was almost eight o'clock. Her pulse rose with excitement. Paul would be awake now. He'd be knocking on her door, wondering where she was.

Hurrying inland from the narrow strip of beach, she made her way back across the sprawling lawns the way she'd come.

It was just as she was turning the corner by

the huge conservatory to the west of the house, that she received a terrible shock.

Standing there in the center of the path, blocking her passage effectively, was the sinister person she'd first set eyes on in Cologne. Her mouth went dry. What was he doing here? How had he followed her movements so accurately?

As it was daylight, Laurel was able to take in much more of the stranger's appearance. The trilby hat still covered most of his face and hair, but she could see he was tall and slender, in almost a feminine way, and that he had slim, tapering hands that were attached to painfully thin wrists.

One of those hands went quickly to the stranger's pocket and she wondered if he was secreting a weapon there.

Willing herself to remain calm, she spoke slightly breathlessly.

"What do you want of me? We don't know each other. Why have you taken the trouble to follow me here?"

The man didn't answer. Instead, he seemed to feast his smoldering eyes malevolently on her, as though gathering more fuel for his hatred.

Just as Laurel thought she might scream through fearful anticipation, the man started to approach her.

Her heart hammered painfully in her breast. She repeated her question more urgently.

"Tell me who you are and what you want?"

At that point the stranger uttered a laugh. It was so high-pitched that Laurel felt sure the man was mentally deranged. At the same time he drew a wicked-looking knife from his pocket and brandished it at her.

"Oh God – no!" Laurel screamed, losing her nerve. "You're mad. Keep away from me. Keep away!"

She turned and ran frantically back across the lawn. She could hear the man's footsteps behind and wondered wretchedly what she would do when she reached the shores of the lake and could go no further.

Darting through the grove of walnuts and hazel trees, she heard the panting breath of her assailant just behind. Then, to her surprise, he uttered a scream.

Though petrified with terror, Laurel turned. It was then she received another surprise. The stranger's trilby hat had come adrift and long, flowing locks of dark hair had escaped, becoming entangled on overhanging branches.

"For God's sake – you're not a man – you're a woman!" Laurel gasped.

"You have stolen my husband!" The woman cried out with such anguish that Laurel almost felt sorry for her.

"I've never met your husband," she shouted back in German.

"Don't lie! Erich is my husband – and you have stolen him from me!"

It was then that so many things became clear in Laurel's mind. This must be the woman who'd escaped from the clinic. Probably, also, the one who hated her sister so intensely. And she had mistaken her for Jenny.

The woman looked so helpless, trapped among the branches like a great black bird, that Laurel felt pity rise for her.

"Oh – help me, please!" the poor mad woman cried. "I am dying of pain. There are claws in these trees that will not let me go."

Without thinking how foolish she was being, Laurel went to the woman's rescue. It was only when she was inches away that she realized she had been duped. The woman had only been pretending to be trapped. As she sprang at Laurel, lifting the hand that contained the knife she gave a shriek of triumph.

"Now we shall see whose heart bleeds most!"

In the split second that the weapon began its descent, Laurel dodged to one side. The point of the blade entered her shoulder and, as blood spurted, she gave a gasp of pain.

The woman's terrible laugh rang out again. Then Laurel heard the sound of branches snapping underfoot as someone raced toward them through the copse.

Paul's voice shouted out and she nearly fainted there and then with relief.

"Hold on, Laurel – I'm coming!"

What happened next was just a painful blur.

She was aware that Paul was grappling with the woman for the knife. Servants from the house came tearing across the lawns. Before long the mad woman had been overpowered, and then Paul was picking Laurel up from where she'd crumpled in a heap, and was trying to stem the flow of blood that seeped through her blouse with his handkerchief.

"Oh, God, Laurel – are you all right? I heard you screaming. Someone's fetching a doctor. I'll carry you up to the house. Everything will be all right. My God, if you die, I'll never forgive myself for doubting your story."

She was dimly aware of his strong arms lifting her into the air. And then the scent of the soap he'd used that morning was in her nostrils as he carried her across the lawn.

To add to the confusion, Jenny and Erich arrived by ambulance from Zurich at the same time as the doctor got there to attend to Laurel. It was some time later before calm descended once more in the Camathias household.

The doctor had bound her shoulder in a sling and ordered rest for Laurel. Other than that, he had reassured them, the wound was not as deep as they'd at first feared. She had lost some blood, but she was young and strong and would soon make it up again over the next twenty-four hours.

"It never rains but it pours," Jenny said, putting her arm around her sister's good shoulder affectionately. "Now I've two patients to nurse instead of one."

Laurel glanced over to where Erich lay on a couch in the morning sunshine, looking pale but filled with love for her sister. Paul was sitting in an easy chair, looking slightly out of things. She gave him a special smile to bring him back in.

"Two peas in a pod," he murmured. "How am I ever going to tell you apart?"

"You will find ways," Erich told him. "For a start, Jenny has this little mole – "

"Not now!" Jenny warned him.

"If you mean the one she has on her leg, I have one in the same position," Laurel put in.

"No – I mean a different one somewhere else," he said quietly.

To break the embarrassing silence, Jenny said –

"What I shall never understand is how you found your way here if you never received that letter I sent."

"With great difficulty," Paul told her.

"I'm quite sure. But how?"

"Through that newspaper cutting of Hohengrünfeld," Laurel said.

"Hohen what?"

"Hohengrünfeld – you remember, you cut it out of a newspaper. I found it with that photo of Erich and you in one of your pockets."

Jenny grew even more mystified. "But I've

never heard of the place. Have you got the cutting with you now?"

"*I* have it," Paul said, putting his hand in his pocket and bringing it out.

Jenny took it from him, unfolding it and frowning. "But this is ridiculous. I don't remember cutting this out." After a few seconds she turned it over. It was then she gave a sigh of understanding. "*This* is what I cut it out for – the page of hospital appointments." She began to explain. "At one time, before I accepted Erich's proposal, I thought of changing my job. I kept this cutting purely for the telephone number of another clinic."

Laurel could barely believe the coincidence. "Then you mean you didn't even know the picture of Hohengrünfeld was on the other side?"

"I've already told you so."

Paul glanced at Erich enquiringly. "And you, Doctor Camathias? You're completely unaware of any connection?"

He shook his head. "I am as much bemused as Jenny."

Paul gave a frown. "Then I can only say that fate has the weirdest sense of humor. Without this cutting we would never have managed to locate you – "

"And Paul and I may never have met again – "

He captured Laurel's eyes. "I think we would."

"But how can you say that?" she insisted. "We met purely and simply because we happened to catch the same train to Stuttgart – "

"Will someone please put Erich and me in the picture?" Jenny interrupted impatiently.

After Paul had told them all they had learned at the house in Stuttgart Jenny and Erich were amazed.

"But this is incredible," he said. "I had no idea of this connection. I was only aware that my grandmother, who died young, was incredibly beautiful by her family portrait, and that neither my father nor myself resembled her in any way." He grew pensive. "It seems the man I called my grandfather, who died when I was a child, was her second husband, and not really my grandfather at all."

"Do you think there might also be some link between the von Haagen household and the poor mad woman at the clinic? Laurel asked thoughtfully.

"Why on earth should you think that?" Jenny enquired in surprise.

Laurel shook her head. "It was just something she said." She frowned, trying to remember. "She said – you have stolen my husband. Erich is my husband and you have stolen him from me – "

Jenny shook her head sadly. "Poor confused woman. Evidently she had a thing on Erich. It's not unknown for people to get crushes on their shrinks." She shuddered. "In that case it was the reason she hated me so much – and the reason she followed you here, Laurel, mistaking you for me."

"What will happen to her now?" Paul asked with interest.

"The ambulance that brought Erich and me here from Zurich will take her back to Constance. From there she'll be taken back over the German border and returned to the clinic in Cologne."

"Surely that's unwise. What if she escapes again?"

"More care will be taken. And, now that we know what was making her worse, someone will help her to come to terms with it. But you may want to prefer a charge against her, Laurel? You've every right to."

"You know I don't. In spite of what she did, I can feel only pity for her."

The rest of the day was spent quietly. Although she was longing to be alone with Paul, there seemed to be so much that she and Jenny had to discuss.

It was only during the next morning, that Paul, who had spent most of the time since Laurel's accident on his own, asked –

"Are you feeling up to taking a short drive, Laurel?"

She agreed gladly. She had missed his company abysmally. Much as she had been interested in learning Jenny's plans for the future, and the hospital's prognosis where Erich was concerned, she was longing, even more, to know what Paul might have in mind for *their* future.

As they walked toward the car, she touched his arm.

"Let's walk down to the lake instead," she said.

He nodded, slightly absent-mindedly. Then he took her hand and they wandered slowly down to the shore.

For a long time he was silent. She imagined him trying to put his feelings for her into words. She longed for the moment when he would hold her and tell her how much he loved her. So sure was she of her own feelings for him that she was completely unprepared for what came next.

He gave a sigh. "I've had plenty of time to think about what happened the other night, Laurel. And I'm afraid one of us may have been rushing into things."

Her heart went cold.

"In what – in what way do you mean?" she stammered.

"Rebounds are funny things," he said with a shrug. "Often a person tends to think they're falling in love when all the time they're not. Love and infatuation can be very confusing."

She remembered his earlier warning on the first night they arrived there. Slowly she drew her hand from his.

"We really needn't have walked so far just for you to tell me that."

He looked back and saw the distance they'd come.

"Oh, God – how selfish can a person get?" he asked, angry at himself. "I'm forgetting how weak you must still be feeling. Forgive me – let me put my arm around you. We'll sit on this log and you can rest."

She shook his arm away.

Standing, pale-faced through the shock of his words, her arm still in its protective sling, she stared at him with dignity.

"I'm not a bit tired – or weak. In fact, I shall soon be right as rain again. The doctor said – " she broke off, aware that she was talking to stop herself from thinking. Never once in her life had she been a coward. She must face up to the fact that he no longer loved her.

"What I suggest, Paul," she went on without looking at him, "is that you say what you brought me out here to say, and stop beating about the bush."

He looked down at her, trying to measure the length of her dark lashes with his eyes. "That's just about it. I mean – all I had to say. I thought I'd bring it up in good time and let you dwell on it."

For some time she stared out across the lake at the little town the other side, forcing herself not to burst into tears and make an idiot of herself. What Paul was trying to say, and not very skillfully or honestly, she told herself, was that he had never been in love with her. He was still in love with Fern, his dead fiancée. He had merely allowed his emotions to get the better of him when he'd held her in his arms and whispered all those things the evening they'd found the house.

At length she plucked up courage to reply, trying to keep the bitterness from her tone.

"I don't think there's anything to dwell on. People make mistakes. That's all there is to it." She smiled at him. "How wise you were. And thank goodness we didn't allow this infatuation to go any further. One of us might have got badly hurt."

A small pulse beat at the side of his temple. His blue eyes were narrowed as though he was having difficulty seeing through the sunlight.

He swallowed. "You can say that again," he said quietly.

Silence descended between them like a deadening blanket. It lengthened into what seemed an eternity, during which she told herself what a fool she'd been to ever delude herself into thinking he was fond of her. She should have realized, after all he'd told her in the breakfast room at Constance, that anything between them, on his side, would be nothing more than momentary infatuation.

She heard him breathe a sigh, drawing the air up painfully from somewhere deep inside his chest.

"Well, Laurel – I guess now we've sorted that out, it leaves very little for us to say to each other."

"How right you are," she murmured, turning her head so that he wouldn't notice her tears if she found she could no longer control them. "And please don't think you have to stay with me, simply because I've hurt my shoulder. If you must know, I'd much prefer to be left here on my own. I'd like you to go back to the house. I shall be perfectly all right."

"I couldn't possibly do that. Don't ask me to, Laurel. It's only right you should let me accompany you back – "

"Oh, go – go, Paul Troughton – " she said furiously, losing the tenuous hold she had on her emotions. "I want to be left alone to think."

He stayed a further moment before giving in. "Very well – if it's really what you want. But I'll take the precaution of sending Jenny down in half an hour if you haven't returned – "

"Oh, damn you! just go – go! Leave me in peace."

10

Laurel stayed down by the shore of Lake Constance for a long time; her heart, that had been as light as thistledown two days ago, now as heavy as lead.

How was it possible, she asked herself bitterly, for someone to be in love one minute and out of it the next? What had she done to make Paul change so completely? Was she so utterly repellent that she drove men away? First Gavin – and now Paul.

"Hi!" her sister called, emerging from the grove without Laurel hearing. "Paul told me you were here all on your own but I couldn't come before. I had to settle Erich and give him some physiotherapy the hospital insists on. But I could see you were OK from the bedroom window." She paused, before going on somewhat cautiously. "Incidentally, your friend has left. Was that arranged between the two of you, or have you had a tiff?"

"Neither," Laurel told her shortly. "It seems he came to his senses, and obviously thought the best thing he could do was take himself off."

"And how about you? Is that what you wanted?"

"Don't ask," Laurel replied tearfully. "I'm not quite sure what I feel at this moment – anger distorts everything."

"Oh, poor love," Jenny said sympathetically, putting her arm round her. "Cry on my shoulder, if it helps. I know what it's like to break up with someone. I didn't tell you before, but I was badly let down by someone just before I fell in love with Erich. It was the thing I wanted to chat about when I last called you. But you sounded so busy – "

"Oh, I've become so selfish," Laurel said, putting her hand over her eyes. "I remember – I was so wrapped up in my own misery over Gavin at the time that I couldn't be bothered to listen to what you had to say."

Jenny grimaced. "That's what comes of being identical twins. Astrology tells us we tend to suffer the same experiences at the same time."

"But you recovered sufficiently to become engaged to Erich so soon after?"

"Yes – but I'd known him a long time. I'd been winter-sporting with him along with other friends, and I saw him at the clinic most days. Nevertheless, I still thought it might be a rebound effect. That's why I wanted to chat things over with you. I've always had great respect for your opinions." She stared pensively into the distance. "But I know I was right in accepting Erich's proposal, now. Believe it or not, it was infatuation I'd felt for the *other* person." She smiled. "I realize that, now that my love's been tried and tested by that accident. I really thought I'd die when he was so ill."

Tears ran down Laurel's face at the same time as they ran down her sister's.

"And I knew nothing of all this," she sobbed. "You must have thought me such a heartless brute."

"No – I blame myself entirely for not having the sense to call instead of write. And what about all the worry I've given *you* – having to come all this way to find me? And only by the wildest of coincidences, too." She paused. "You know – Erich and I have been talking about that. It was evidently a heaven-sent sign. And he's going to follow up what you told us. No matter what his grandfather did – sending his wife away – it seems a pity he should be left to live out the last days of his life with only that old dragon of a housekeeper you told us about for company."

They walked back to the house and she asked –

"What will you do now – about Paul, I mean?"

Laurel shook her head emphatically. "Nothing at all. At least I've still got my pride. He'll never know if I really loved him or not. For all he can tell, it could have been rebound on *my* part, too."

"And are you quite sure it isn't?"

Laurel took her time replying.

"Yes," she said softly. "Just as *you* did, I know now that what I felt for Gavin was infatuation. What I feel for Paul – well – it's something – something completely different."

Later that evening she asked Jenny if she could call Derrick.

Her sister laughed. "This is your home for as long as you want to stay here. Call who you please. By the way, Erich and I have decided to get married as soon a possible, while you're still down here. It'll save the upset of having to take a plane to England while his back is on the mend. So please don't make arrangements to leave just yet."

"I'm pleased for both of you," Laurel told her. "But I think I should let Derrick know, and ask him if everything's all right at the shop."

Jenny nodded. "I'll leave you to it, then. Erich and I have masses to talk about now that we're bringing our wedding plans forward – "

Laurel turned her head as Jenny started to discuss them with her. Her younger sister by five minutes had never been the epitome of tact. If only Jenny knew how much it hurt, flinging her own happiness with Erich in her face.

When Laurel at last managed to get through to Derrick's number to tell him her search was at an end, he told her how fortunate she was to catch him at home.

"How's that?" she asked. "I thought you were very much a home bird?"

"That's all in the past," he laughed. "I've now decided that life has been passing me by at far too fast a pace. So I'm doing something about it."

"You're not chasing women, I hope?" she said, teasing him, trying to sound cheerful.

"Women! Good Lord, no. Just one."

"Who's that?" she asked curiously.

"No one you know, my dear. I'll introduce you when you come home," he went on, teasing her back. "It's all your fault, old thing. You should have snapped me up while the going was good. I'm afraid you've missed your chance now."

"It seems all my chances are passing me by," she sighed.

"Well, don't sound so heart-broken. I'm sure your turn will come again soon. Oh, incidentally – how have you and Paul been getting along?"

She gave a gasp and the line went silent while she took in what he'd just said.

"Are you there, Laurel? I hope we haven't been cut off."

She was slow reassuring him. "No, I'm still here. Go on with what you were saying about Paul."

"Paul Troughton – he *did* manage to catch

you up, I hope. I phoned him after I'd booked your flight and asked him to act as chaperon. I wasn't too keen on your gallivanting around the Continent all on your own. And he owed me a favor. I was always covering for him and getting him out of scrapes when we were at university. When I heard he was at a loose end, just back from America, I thought the least he could do, to wipe the slate clean, would be to keep an eye on you for me – "

"Thank you for telling me all that, Derrick," she broke in dangerously. "You've simply made my day. Have you anything else to add? The shop hasn't gone bankrupt, has it? My flat hasn't burnt down? Maybe my stocks have reached rock-bottom – "

"What's up?" he asked in a surprised voice. "I've never heard you sound so fed-up before."

"I'm sorry – don't lose any sleep over it – I've got to hang up now. Expect me back in about a week. I'm waiting for a stab wound to heal. Jenny's getting married. And I'm staying to be the specter at the feast."

After she'd put the receiver back in its cradle she stared at her reflection in the mirror across the living-room. Two angry spots of color had risen in her cheeks.

So that was it! She'd often suspected something like it. Their "accidental" meetings had always seemed far too much of a coincidence. Taking the seat next to her on the plane – the mix-up over the taxi – her running into him again at the bus-stop. And then, to cap it all, the way he'd burst onto the train.

Paul had been doing everything purely as a favor to Derrick. Keeping his eye on her.

She bowed her head, trying to rid her memory of how gullible she'd been. Then she faced her reflection again.

Doing all those things, she told herself furiously. And so much more. Letting her fall in love with him. Allowing her to think he was following her of his own accord because he'd grown fond of her

And now Derrick had finally burst her bubble.

God – what an idiot Paul must have thought her. Her senses reeled as she remembered the night they'd shared his room in Constance. Would he tell Derrick about that? Would they laugh together like schoolboys over the episode?

Et tu, Derrick, she thought scornfully. Her partner for the past two years! The guy who'd shared all her business ups and downs. The one she'd always thought of as a loyal friend. He had actually been the instigator of this plot against her. It was almost unbelievable.

11

It was pouring with rain when Laurel landed at Heathrow Airport a week later. She thought of the sunshine she'd left behind in Switzerland and almost wished she was still there.

But all holidays had to come to an end sometime, she told herself. Even a holiday where she had spent a large portion of each day on her own, walking in solitude around the lake, trying to come to terms with herself and where her life was leading.

In a way, the thing Derrick had told her had made it slightly easier to turn her love for Paul into contempt. Scorn was easier to keep up than self-pity.

Jenny and Erich had been married the day before. It hadn't been a large affair. And they had decided to defer the honeymoon until Erich was entirely well.

"Life's a honeymoon here," Jenny said happily, handing her simple wedding bouquet of Swiss mountain flowers and tiny red rosebuds over to Laurel. "And now it's your turn. You remember what astrology tells us about identical twins following similar patterns?"

"I've already decided I'll be an old maid,"

Laurel said. "You and Erich will have masses of children, and I'll be the crotchety old aunt who comes to stay at regular intervals."

"No way," Jenny laughed. "What's the betting you'll be planning a wedding yourself within the next few months?"

"The way I'm feeling at the moment," Laurel told her testily, "I should say the odds are practically nil."

She thought about that again as she unlocked the door of her apartment. Looking around, she remembered the bitter tears she'd cried there over Gavin. Was that really so short a while ago?

And now, here she was with another heartful of ache over someone else. If she wasn't careful she would quickly earn a reputation for being a flirt. Except that no one would ever know about Paul – unless *he* did the talking.

Among the pile of business mail on the mat was a hand-posted letter with large untidy writing. She opened it first.

It was short and had no address.

I guessed you might find it difficult picking up the things you left at your hotel in Cologne. Since I was the one with the car, I called there on my way back. You'll find your case with the hall porter.

Good luck in all you do. Thanks for a lot of memories.

Paul.

The fact that he'd written stunned her. Why had he bothered to do anything so considerate?

It was true. She had wondered how she'd be able to pick the case up. It would have meant catching one plane to Cologne and then another from there to London, instead of the one she eventually caught from Zurich. After talking it over with her sister they'd agreed that she or Erich would collect it and bring it over to England at a later date. Now, through Paul's charitable act, the necessity had been canceled out.

Maybe he thought he owed her that much, she thought coldly.

When she went into the shop next morning, Derrick greeted her affectionately with a friendly kiss.

"Look at that – roses back in your cheeks." He smiled. "That break's done you a power of good, Laurel. It's blown away all your apathy. You're looking really great."

"Then you must try it yourself some time," she said over-sweetly. "And *I'll* put a watchdog on *your* tail and we'll see how you like it."

He looked worried. "That's what I don't understand. I thought you and Paul would have got along famously. He's a great guy to have around – "

"If you promise never to mention his name to me again, then I'll promise not to tell this girlfriend of yours all the embarrassing things I know about you. Is that a deal?"

"I suppose so. But I still don't understand – "

She interrupted firmly. "When am I going to meet this paragon of virtue who's managed to send you all starry-eyed, anyway?"

"Shortly," he said. "She'll probably be coming in to the shop later today. She's interested to meet you." He paused. "I'd say you and she have a lot in common."

"What's that supposed to mean?"

He grew embarrassed. "I'm sorry – I've just remembered – I've got an early appointment with our accountant. We'll carry on with this conversation some other time."

She watched him rush off. Then she went up to her office, hoping life wasn't going to be too hectic too soon. She'd grown used to her own company over the past seven days.

By the time coffee break came she was already well back into routine. She'd arranged a fashion show for later in the month, had taken a sneak preview at the latest styles, had selected two girls as likely models from a pile of CVs and photographs, and arranged for Derrick to see them.

Just before lunch her secretary called from the outer office to tell her that one of the prospective models had arrived at the shop and would shortly be coming up to be interviewed.

"Then show her into Derrick's office," Laurel

said. "You know he likes to make the final choice."

"I think he's got someone else there, at the moment. Shall I keep her here when they send her up, and give her some magazines to read? Oh – by the way, will it be all right if I go to lunch as soon as she gets here? I've promised my boyfriend I'll meet him."

"Yes, all right – oh, which girl is it? Sally Flint or Fiona Scales?"

"Fiona," her secretary replied.

It was almost a quarter of an hour later before Laurel could leave her office. The other phone rang just as she replaced the receiver from talking to Cheryl. It was a call from Paris and a very important one.

At last she was able to get away and opened the door of the outer office with an apology ready on her lips for the young woman, if she was still waiting there. But it was wasted on fresh air. The model had either got tired of waiting and left, since Cheryl's pile of magazines looked as though they'd been recently thumbed through, or Derrick's visitor had left and he'd found her waiting there.

Laurel gave a shrug. Such was life. If it was the former she would have to go through the pile of CVs again and pick someone else. There was always a heavy waiting list for such a plum job.

As she went down the wide staircase into the main part of the shop, she happened to look through the plate-glass doors into the busy street and her heart did a swift somersault. There on the sidewalk, talking earnestly to a tall, slender and fantastically elegant young woman, was the man she'd last seen on the shores of Lake Constance.

Her legs went weak beneath her. Paul Troughton had his arm around the girl's shoulder in an intimate fashion. The jealousy Laurel experienced had no right to be there, in view of the times she'd told herself how much she despised him.

She brushed a nervous hand over her forehead. Maybe that had never been the truth. Perhaps, in spite of everything, she was still as much in love with him as she'd always been.

But, if that was the case, the next moment told her how hopeless that love was. Before her eyes, he kissed the attractive woman and got into a car parked nearby, driving off at the same time as his girlfriend entered the shop.

Laurel stood rooted to the spot. Then, through the buzz of noise that came up from below, she heard the woman ask for Derrick, saying she had an appointment.

Laurel gasped. It was the missing model, Fiona.

Without anyone seeing, she returned quickly up the stairs. There, standing nervously in the outer office, wringing her hands, she wondered what she could possibly do.

It was out of the question to offer the young

woman a position with the firm after what she'd witnessed. Even apart from her feelings of jealousy, it would be unbearable to have Paul calling there each day at the shop to bring her, or pick her up. She would have to put Derrick in the picture and plead with him to say the position was no longer vacant.

Opening the door of his office, her heart sank when she found he was no longer there.

Footsteps sounded just behind, trapping her before she could escape. She turned slowly and saw the woman she'd seen with Paul giving her a friendly smile.

Close to, she was even lovelier than her photograph. So many of the models they employed had a certain sameness about them. This one was quite different. About twenty-one – a natural blonde – fresh, and as slender as a lily. Laurel's jealously increased. She would have a hard job getting Derrick to turn her down. She would just have to do it herself without him knowing.

"Can I help you?" she asked distantly. "My name is Laurel Brownridge. I'm afraid my partner, Derrick Hanley, isn't available at the moment."

"So you're Laurel Brownridge!" The model came forward with a smile, putting out her hand. "I've heard so much about you. It's extremely nice to meet you at last."

Laurel pretended not to notice the outstretched hand.

"Yes, Laureder's getting quite well known," she replied.

"I didn't quite mean – "

"Would you like to come inside and take a seat? I'm sure you won't mind if I do the interviewing instead of Mr Hanley. And, by the way, I've got some bad news, I'm afraid. The vacancy we thought we had came up on our computer in error. I can put your CV back on the file again for a later date, but I'm afraid we can't offer you anything at the present moment."

"There must be some mistake – "

"I agree. It's all the fault of a junior member of our staff. But these things happen sometimes in the best of businesses. I can only apologize on behalf of our firm and, as I said, bear your name in mind if a genuine vacancy occurs shortly – "

The young woman opposite studied her as though she was talking gibberish and had taken leave of her senses.

"I'm really very sorry – " Laurel finished lamely.

"As I said – I think there's some mistake. We're probably talking at cross purposes – "

"I don't think so," Laurel said, hardening her tone. "Your name is Fiona, am I right?"

"That's so but – "

"Then there's nothing left to say. Good afternoon, Miss Scales. I'm sorry the vacancy isn't available."

As Laurel got up from Derrick's desk, bringing the interview to a close, he came into the room. With a pleased smile, he looked from one to the other. Then he went straight up to Fiona and kissed her warmly on the cheek.

His voice was breathless. "Gosh, I'm sorry I wasn't around when you arrived, love. But, at least it's given you and Laurel a chance to get to know each other."

"I don't think so," Fiona laughed. "Actually I was just being told in no uncertain terms that the job I'd applied for was no longer available."

"What job?" He looked puzzled.

"Heaven knows!"

"You told me your name was Fiona Scales," Laurel accused.

"Fiona – yes. Scales – no." The woman shook her head.

Laurel sighed and put her hand up to her forehead. "I'm really very sorry. I must be going mad. You'll both have to excuse me. I have an appointment with a client for lunch, and I'm already late. By the way, Derrick, I'll be going straight back to Maddox's afterward, to see their new accessories."

"In that case, I'll see you in the morning, old thing."

That evening Laurel sat alone in her apartment, staring at a dull television program and wondering what she could do about the awkward situation that seemed to have arisen.

In spite of the fact that Derrick was so smitten with his new girlfriend, there was no mistaking the intimate way she had observed her and Paul behaving. It was clear they knew each other extremely well.

She had no desire to see Derrick made a fool of. But, if she put him in the picture, he might say it was just sour grapes on her part. And wasn't it? Wasn't she more concerned with how bitter she felt than how silly Derrick might feel?

Why couldn't life be simple?

It was at that moment the phone rang. She got up to answer it. Perhaps it was Jenny, wanting to find out if she'd settled back to work all right?

But it wasn't. It was Derrick.

"Hi!" she said, slightly taken aback. "What are you doing calling me out of working hours? Don't we put in enough time with each other during the day?"

"It has nothing to do with business. Anyway, can't a friend call a friend whenever he likes?"

"I suppose so. If he's nothing better to do. Where's Fiona?" she asked guardedly.

"She's the person I'm calling about."

"Oh, really. Well, I can assure you she's not here."

"Stop trying to be funny, Laurel," he said in a unusually serious tone. I've something to tell you. I'd have told you earlier if you hadn't made things difficult for me."

"Oh, indeed!"

"Yes – well – "

"Do go on."

"Not now. I'm quite a coward at heart. Especially when you get a bee in your bonnet about someone. Look – what I want you to do is come to a rock concert with me."

"A what?"

"A rock concert, my girl. I'm afraid your education's been sadly lacking in some things."

She tried to get out of it.

"I really don't think I'll enjoy that, Derrick. I much prefer my music less rowdy and a whole lot sweeter. I'm very much a middle of the road person – "

"Stop arguing and do something to please me. I promise you might even learn something to your advantage."

"And what's that?"

"Do as I say and come out with me. I'll pick you up in half an hour. Oh – and don't bother to dress. It's strictly a jeans and gumboots do – "

"Where's this concert taking place?" she asked sarcastically. "In the middle of a field?"

"Something like that." He gave a laugh. "I'll be around as soon as I can."

you. I'd have told you earlier if you hadn't made things difficult for me."

"Oh indeed!"

"Yes – well –"

"Do go on."

"Not now. I'm quite a coward at heart, especially when you get a bee in your bonnet about someone. Look – what I want you to do is come to a rock concert with me."

"A what?"

"A rock concert, my girl. I'm afraid your education's been sadly lacking in some things."

She tried to get out of it.

"I really don't think I'll enjoy that, Derrick. I much prefer my music less rowdy and a whole lot sweeter. I'm very much a middle of the road person –"

"Stop arguing and do something to please me! I promise you might even learn something to your advantage."

"And what's that?"

"Do as I say and come out with me. I'll pick you up in half an hour. Oh – and don't bother to dress. It's strictly a jeans and jumpers do."

"Where's this concert taking place?" she asked sarcastically. "In the middle of a field?"

"Something like that." He gave a laugh. "I'll be around as soon as I can."

12

Standing in the reception area of her smart block of apartments, shivering slightly in the cool night air, Laurel waited for Derrick to arrive, wondering whether he'd taken leave of his senses. She'd never known him to have any interest in rock concerts before.

Then a fantastic thought arose. Maybe his girlfriend, Fiona, was a pop singer. She had looked so well-groomed and so attractive it probably wasn't out of the question. Although, from what she'd seen in magazines and on television, it might prove to be a set-back in such a career.

Just before the half-hour was up, Derrick arrived in his smart car.

He opened the door for her to get in. They were alone. There was no sign of Fiona.

"Where are we really going?" she asked.

"To a rock concert. I thought I told you."

"You did. And I admire your line of humor. Will you please tell me whether April Fool's Day has changed its position this year?"

He ignored the question and took a swift glance down at her shoes.

"I hope you're wearing something sturdy.

Grass can get very muddy at this time of year – "

"You're not really serious about it being in the open air, are you?" she enquired incredulously.

"Absolutely!" He gave a laugh. "And now sit back and watch the lights of the city fade behind as we head for deep country."

Deep country turned out to be the grounds of a fine country mansion in the green belt of Surrey.

When Laurel got out of the car she was surprised to see how many other people had gathered there. A marquee had been set up in the grounds, but there was no sign of any rowdiness or bad behavior, which she'd usually connected with such concerts.

The occasion had been extremely well organized. A stage had been erected inside the tent. And a huge monitor screen had been positioned outside to cater for the large overflow of people who were unable to get seats inside the marquee.

A Master of Ceremonies was up on the stage thanking everyone for coming and telling them he hoped they'd raise a terrific amount for charity.

After the preliminaries the concert began to get into its swing.

"Did you have to buy tickets for this?" she

asked Derrick some time later during a short intermission between groups.

He nodded.

"You'll have to let me pay you back. How much were they?"

He named what seemed to her an incredible sum for such a thing and she swallowed.

"Now I know why you asked *me* to come instead of your girlfriend."

"Don't be such a Scrooge," he laughed. "Anyway, it's for a good charity. You'll see Fiona shortly, I hope. *She* didn't have to pay to come in."

Laurel nodded to herself. So she'd been right. Fiona was one of the performers.

In spite of her musical preference being on the classical side, she found she quite enjoyed some of the groups. It was after one in the morning when she realized the concert was about to come to an end and Fiona hadn't yet been on.

"I thought your girlfriend was one of the artists," she said.

"Good Lord – whatever gave you that funny idea?"

"*You* did. You said we'd see her shortly."

He looked about. "That's right. She must be busy. These things take a lot of organizing."

So – she was one of the organizers, Laurel decided. That made more sense. She wondered again what she should do to try to warn him about Paul Troughton's interests.

"You know," she said diplomatically, "I'm not quite sure how attached you are to her, Derrick?"

"I'm in love with her," he admitted. "I always have been."

"But you hardly know her. You only met while I was away."

He shook his head. "I've known her for years. That's why I've never been interested in any other girl."

"Oh!"

She knew now that she could never tell him what she knew. She would hurt him too deeply. She would just have to leave him to find out.

Then she racked her brains hopefully. Maybe there was another explanation? Perhaps she'd grown too narrow-minded over the years. Maybe it was quite in order in these enlightened times, for people to be deeply affectionate with more than one person. But, if that was the case, it wasn't for her. She was old-fashioned enough to want to have someone entirely to herself.

She looked around. The marquee and grounds were beginning to empty at a rapid pace. People were pouring out of the gates on foot, and in fabulously expensive motor cars. Artists were leaving by droves in coaches and mini-buses. Cleaners were already starting to make their rounds, picking up the garbage that was lying about the beautiful gardens and putting it into dozens of plastic bags.

"Ah – here's Fiona now," Derrick announced. "And – and she's got someone else with her – I'm sorry, Laurel, but it's someone you don't particularly care for – "

To Laurel's distress, Paul Troughton was walking beside the lovely young woman. What was more they seemed to be sharing a private joke together. They looked entirely comfortable in each other's company.

Her heart-beats rose at the sight of him. She thought how distinguished he looked, once more dressed in a suit instead of jeans.

He saw her at the same moment. The floodlights had not yet been dismantled. Abruptly he came to a standstill.

Derrick took her hand firmly in his, leading her forward.

"Well, hallo you two. How are the takings? Has anyone counted them yet? Do you think the whole show will have been worth all your efforts?"

Fiona answered. "Very much so, I'd have thought, by the crowds. But, thank goodness, that's not our side of it. Arithmetic was never my strong point." She gave a laugh. "And what do you know, it's all thanks to the efforts of *this* person. I've never seen such freneticism as he's put into everything. You'd have thought the devil incarnate was behind him with a fiery trident, the way he's worked to get the whole thing together in so short a time – "

As she was talking, Laurel took a deeper look at Paul. She thought he looked more worn and tired than she'd ever seen him before.

"You've been burning too much midnight oil, old man," said Derrick, putting her thoughts into words. "What you could use is a holiday – " he broke off looking foolish. "Sorry, I forgot – you've just come back from one."

"What he could use is a good woman," Fiona said, firmly. "Since Fern died he's been an absolute wreck. And now, I suspect someone else has let him down. I've never known anyone so moody and snappish – oh, Laurel Brownridge – I forgot – neither of us has bothered to introduce you. This is my uncle and guardian, Paul Troughton – or Lord Guthrie, really, but he doesn't advertise it – "

All Laurel could do was stare. She had never considered the fact that they might be related. He looked far too young to be Fiona's uncle, let alone guardian. Barely ten years separated their ages. Maybe her parents had been killed in an accident and he'd taken over responsibility for her. Whatever the reason, *now* was not the time for such surmise. Paul was staring back at her, taking in every detail of her expression beneath the lights.

"I'm sorry, Laurel, I didn't realize you were going to be here or I'd have kept out of the way." He went on in a slightly embarrassed fashion. "Did you get your case? I dropped a note in your mailbox. I thought it would save you the trouble of going all the way to Cologne before you came home."

She nodded. "That was very kind of you. But you needn't have taken so much trouble – "

"I can assure you it was no trouble – "

Fiona interrupted them. "So you two already know each other. No one ever tells me a thing. Did *you* know, Derrick?"

"Yes, I knew," he said quietly. "I say, how about taking me into your warm house and making me a cup of coffee to help me thaw out? The dawn will be up soon, I can't say I'm over keen on these late venues."

"You're getting disgustingly old, Derrick. It's not even two yet. But, if you want coffee, I suppose I'll have to make you some. That's what fiancées are for."

She turned to Paul and Laurel who had continued to stare at each other as though they were the only real people in the whole world.

"How about you two? While I'm making for us I might just as well make it for four."

"Not for me," Paul said quietly. "And not for Laurel, either. I want to have a chat with her. It's been over a week since I've seen her."

"But that's impossible. You were in Switzerland then – and Laurel – Laurel was out of the country too – " the penny suddenly dropped.

"Oh, I see," Fiona went on slowly, giving a broad smile. "*That* accounts for a lot."

The floodlights were still illuminating the garden as Paul took Laurel by the arm.

"I'm afraid I've no lake," he said. "But I've a really nice arbor. The honeysuckle there is a picture in early summer." He gave a shrug. "Except it's not early summer now, is it? And you probably wouldn't see much of it even if it was, since the lights will be extinguished soon."

"What are you doing here?" she asked incredulously.

"You mean besides organizing a charity concert? Well, I also happen to live here."

She turned away. "I didn't mean that. I meant what are you doing walking by my side? I didn't expect to find you here. I didn't expect to ever see you again."

"Oh, I'm just like a bad penny. I have a habit of turning up when I'm least expected. How's Gavin, incidentally? Have you managed to extricate him from your system yet?"

"That's uncalled for. You know I never gave him another thought after I met – I mean – after I started my search for Jenny. Anything I'd ever felt for my former fiancé I left behind in England."

"Ah, I see. I had the feeling you might be thinking of picking up the threads again."

"How could I? You're forgetting, it was *he*

who threw me over, not the other way around."

"Ah, yes – that's so. I forgot."

They walked on. She could feel the dampness of the grass seeping in through her inadequate shoes but took no notice. In spite of the fact that Paul had told her he'd only been infatuated with her, it was wonderful to be with him again, feeling the warmth of his arm next to hers.

"My God – " he said suddenly, coming to a standstill. "I forgot to ask – how's your knife wound? Has it left much of a scar?"

"Hardly any." She went on with a touch of her old fire. "I don't scar very easily. You should know that, otherwise I'd have been much more heart-broken when you dropped your bombshell."

"What bombshell? I'm not sure what you're talking about, Laurel."

She sighed. "Oh, don't let's go into it all over again. I'm sorry I brought it up. I promised myself I wouldn't." She paused before going on more heatedly. "But – while we're on the subject of our short sojourn together – why did you never mention the fact that you were only with me because of a favor to Derrick? Why didn't you take the trouble to tell me you were merely paying off a debt?"

He looked deep into her eyes, understanding filtering into his mind.

"Because it wouldn't have been the truth,"

he said. "Even if Derrick had never approached me to keep my eye on you, I would have been happy to do so." He went on more softly, "I love you, Laurel. I loved you from the moment I set eyes on you. Any bargain I made with Derrick was completely beside the point."

"But that's not true. You told me you'd realized you were only infatuated with me. It was just something that was happening on the rebound – "

His eyes grew wide with disbelief. "You've gone dotty, my love. When I took you down to the lake I was warning you that what you felt for *me* might be rebound love. I'd had plenty of time to think about it, left to my own devices while you and your sister spent every minute together, forcing me out in the cold. I couldn't stand any more, especially after your big romance with this Gavin that you were forever thrusting down my throat."

She suddenly saw he was capable of jealousy, too. Her voice became very small.

"But I thought, all the time, that you were telling me you didn't want me."

"Want you!" he exploded. "I've never stopped wanting you. I never shall. You're the only reason I've picked up the pieces again – the reason I want to go on living – "

"But I thought – "

He caught her in his arms and held her tightly.

"Never mind what we both thought. None

of it makes any difference any more. Oh, my God – when I think of the misery we've both been through. I thought I'd go mad when I got back, leaving you there in Switzerland. I had to throw myself into something to keep sane – so I forced myself to put all my efforts into this rock concert Fiona was set on. Never realizing all along, that those efforts would bring you back into my life again."

He kissed her then, tenderly at first and then, with heightened passion, making her heart cry out in ecstasy.

When Laurel opened her eyes again she saw the floodlights had all been extinguished. The night was pitch dark, the moon and stars playing hide and seek behind thick pillars of cloud. Paul's warm breath enflamed her cheek.

"We must be careful," he warned huskily. "I forgot to tell you that my land is pitted by dangerous marshes where deep quicksands lie." He found the curve of her throat and kissed her again, making her gasp with sheer delight. "And, even if we managed to find our way back to the house by skirting the quicksands – we probably wouldn't get through the minefield – "

A smile hovered around her lips as she entered into the spirit of his make-believe.

"Then what do you suggest, Lord Guthrie? I am only a humble village maid, and know not the ways of the gentry."

"I can soon teach you. Fear not. I have a

summer-house not ten feet away. You can spend the night with me there. I can produce signed references for your safe conduct. Do you know, sweet wench, I once spent a night in a room in Constance with the fairest maid in Christendom and never touched one bright hair of her head?"

"Alas, poor maiden." Laurel suppressed a giggle. "How her heart must ache for what she missed?"

Paul tossed make-believe aside.

"What a very naughty Laurel you are," he laughed happily. "I see we shall have some fine winter evenings – after I've made an honest woman of you."